THE *ex* FILES SERIES

EXTORTION

LISA RYAN CAMPBELL

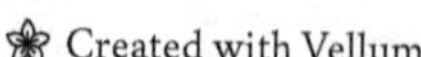 Created with Vellum

*H*ouston, Texas

"You're not answering your phone."

At the sound of her sensual and melodic voice, Drake paused before bringing the glass of scotch and soda to his lips and looked to his right. He wasn't surprised to see her, but he was surprised by the transformation. She'd dressed for the occasion, correctly assuming he'd choose a fancy bar like the St. Regis to drown his thoughts rather than some seedy dive bar on the edge of town.

Instead of the no-nonsense, dark-colored pantsuits she normally wore, she'd shown up in a form-fitting black dress with a V-neck that dipped just low enough to give him a teasing view of her cleavage. She'd replaced the casual loafers with black peep-toe stilettos. She usually styled her hair in a typical French roll or high bun, but tonight, she'd let her hair out, and her natural curls framed her chestnut face and accentuated the dark brown eyes he secretly admitted he loved looking into.

But despite how delectable she looked, he couldn't stand the sight of her and was ready for this toxic relationship of theirs to end. Every time he looked at her, it only reminded him of his betrayal.

"I came here to be alone," he said, taking a sip of his drink.

The dark amber liquid burned as it coated his throat, but he welcomed it as a temporary respite from the constant burden he was carrying.

"I'm sure you did," Cecily said, signaling the bartender. "But let me keep you company for just a moment, and then I'll leave."

Irritation rose inside of him as she placed her clutch on the bar top and scooted herself into the chair beside him.

"Why are you following me?" He asked.

"Well, I would've been here sooner, but I don't have a private jet to zip me anywhere in the world at a moment's notice."

"That's not an answer to my question."

The bartender appeared, and she politely requested a seltzer with lime. Neither of them said a word for the few minutes it took the bartender to make her drink and serve it to her. She thanked him, took a small sip and set it down in front of her. Only then did she turn to look at Drake.

"I'm just concerned."

He put down his glass of scotch with an audible thud, his alone time now ruined.

"Bullshit. You're here to check up on your investment and to make sure we still have a deal."

She didn't answer that, which told him he'd guessed correctly.

"What do you want from me?" He asked. "Edmund's dead, so what business do you and I still have?"

"First, I wanted to offer my condolences."

He scoffed. "Keep your condolences. You don't give a fuck about my family."

"I'm not heartless, Drake."

"What do you want?" He asked again, his patience running thin.

"I followed you here to Texas to tell you that despite Edmund's untimely death, there's still a way for both you and I to get what we want."

"Which is?"

She hesitated. "Marriage."

He had to admit that response gave him pause and slightly intrigued him. "What about it?"

"I want in the family. I want you to marry me."

He gaped at her and then without warning, expelled a burst of laughter. "You're out of your mind."

A slow smile spread across her full lips. "No, I'm desperate. We've been at this for over a year, and we're no closer to finding that money."

"Get to the point where I should care," he said, his voice tinged with sarcasm.

He noticed her fists clench at her sides. It wasn't easy for her to ask for help.

"I have evidence about a murder cover up," she said.

Drake's eyes narrowed. "What are you talking about? What cover-up and what evidence?"

"Documents, recordings, emails," Cecily said. "Anything and everything a DA would need to conduct an investigation. It happened when Edmund was CEO, and the evidence directly links him to the murder."

Drake shrugged even though the actions of Edmund disgusted him. "My brother is gone, so if you want to waste your time going after a dead man, knock yourself out."

Cecily sighed. "Look, Edmund may be dead, but even rumors of a murder investigation would be a PR nightmare for a company with the goal of going public."

He picked up the glass and swallowed another gulp of his

drink, hating that she knew so much about the company and his plans for it.

She leaned in closer and spoke loud enough for only him to hear. "It also wouldn't be good if word got out that Morgan Global Solutions may be hiding money in offshore accounts. I need time to find the money and whoever Edmund's partner is. They're still out there, and my guess is they're working for the company. They might even be in your family. I need to get close to them, and the best way to do that is to pose as your wife."

Drake turned to look at her. She was close enough that he could smell the fragrant perfume she was wearing. He also noticed that her brown skin had traces of freckles along the right side of her cheek. How had he not seen them before?

He looked away just before he lost himself in her gaze.

"I have an entire accounting department to help me find the funds and Edmund's partner."

"And they still haven't found either one, yet."

"And what makes you think you can?"

"I'm good at what I do. I can find that money, and being your wife gives me free reign to your database and to your family. Once I do, I'm gone. Six months tops. By the time this is all over, you'll be free to take the company public. Isn't six months of an inconvenient marriage worth that to you?"

Yes, it was, and she knew it.

"So, what you're saying is if I don't agree to marry you, your next call would be to the DA about Edmund's dirty laundry and possibly the media."

She sat back and had the grace to look chagrined. "You know I don't want to do that."

"But you will. Right?"

He glared at her, silently forcing her to admit that she would do anything to find that money, even extort marriage out of him.

She glared back and grudgingly bit the word out. "Yes."

He chuckled and downed the rest of his scotch in one swallow.

"So, what's it going to be?" She asked with impatience. "I need to get back to San Francisco."

"So soon? You made the trip all the way out here. Why not make the most of it?"

Cecily narrowed her eyes. "What are you talking about?"

"I have a suite upstairs. We've known each other for over a year. Don't tell me you haven't thought about the two of us at least once."

She grabbed her clutch and shifted off the barstool. "I think you've had more than enough to drink."

He grabbed her wrist before she could walk away. "I'm not drunk. I'm sober and thinking very clearly." He paused to look her up and down with derision, but inside, he was turned on by her curves filling out that dress. "Why else would you show up here dressed to kill?"

She leaned into his face to whisper. Her lips were so close, he could taste her if he wanted to. "Like you said, I'm checking on my investment."

"Let's go upstairs," he commanded.

He didn't know what had emboldened him to talk to her that way. Maybe it was the flood of emotions he was feeling —grief mixed with relief that Edmund was gone and anxiety that he'd become the leader of his family's company overnight. He had a lot of work to undo that had been going on for years under Edmund's leadership. It was his job to turn things around, but right now, he had other things— more carnal things—on his mind.

It was true he couldn't stand to be around her, but it didn't stop him from fantasizing about her body and how good she would, no doubt, taste.

She cocked her head to the side and narrowed her eyes

even further until her long lashes became slits. "Are you seriously propositioning me?"

"Yes, I am, and you won't say no. Not if you want me to agree to this whole marriage farce."

"So, this is quid pro quo. That's sexual harassment, Drake."

"Then it's a good thing I'm not your boss. I'm going to be your husband."

He tightened his grip on her wrist and pulled her into him until she was trapped between his parted legs. Her eyes widened at the abrupt move, and before she could stop herself, she had to place her hands against his chest to steady herself. Her lips parted, ready to tell him off, but he silenced her words by encircling his arms around her waist and pulling her in closer to the point that her middle was caressing his groin. He resisted the urge to groan.

"I may have wanted you from the moment I first saw you, but don't mistake this for anything more," he said. "I'm only agreeing to this for my company and my family. Find the money, hand over that evidence so I can destroy it and then get the hell out of my life."

He shoved her away, and if she had feelings, he would've sworn by the look in her eyes he'd bruised them a little. But she didn't have feelings. She was cold as ice, and he was now more eager than ever to get her upstairs, melt it away and see just how hot she could get.

CHAPTER ONE

*S*an Francisco, California
Three weeks later…

Drake fastened the cufflinks of his white dress shirt and surveyed his appearance in the full-length mirror. The smoky gray formal suit fit him to perfection and although he was used to the style and grace of a tailored suit, he felt uncomfortable. His bride-to-be was getting dressed in the adjoining private suite, and he wondered if she was feeling just as detached as him.

For any other couple, this would be a joyous event, but for him, this was just another business deal—a cold and calculated move, a strategic partnership between two people with their own agendas.

The double doors to the penthouse hotel suite swung open. Drake turned from his pensive reflection just as his father and Leo strode in. He held back an exasperated sigh, already knowing why they were here, and it wasn't for well wishes.

"You two might as well save it," he said, grabbing the black tie from the bed and putting it around his neck.

"Too bad because we're not leaving until you hear what we have to say," Leo said. "You come home one day to tell us you're getting married to someone that no one in the family has ever met, and we're not supposed to question it?"

Ivan gave Leo a scolding look and then turned to Drake with a more level tone. "We're just concerned, son."

Concerned. That was the word Cecily used when she trailed him to Houston just before extorting a marriage proposal out of him.

"Well, stop being concerned," he said. "I know what I'm doing."

Ivan nodded, took the tie from Drake's hands and began tying it for him. "After Jasmine, I hoped you'd find someone else and take a chance on love and marriage again. Your mother and I married for love, and I hoped the same for my sons."

"It's just a piece of paper," Drake said.

"Not to me, it isn't." Ivan straightened the knot of the tie and stepped back. "You're treating this like a business arrangement, and you won't tell us why."

Drake turned back to the mirror to look himself over. "I have my reasons. You're just going to have to trust me."

That answer didn't please Ivan in the least. Through his reflection, Drake saw the war in his father's eyes as he struggled between the need to interfere with his son's affairs and letting it all go. In the end, he lovingly slapped Drake on the back and smiled.

"Congratulations, son." Then he turned and left the suite without another word.

Leo stood by the large picture window, appearing to admire the downtown view. But as soon as the doors closed, he rounded on Drake.

"Dad may be willing to let this go, but I'm not. Who is this woman and what does she have on you that you agreed to make her a part of this family?"

"It's just business, Leo."

"Well, if it's just business then why, as your COO, was I not a part of this business arrangement?"

"Because it's got nothing to do with you. She and I came to an agreement and marriage was the result. End of story."

"You never answered me," Leo pressed. "Who is she?"

Drake sighed, turned around and decided to give his brother a half-truth. "I met her one night at a hotel in Houston. It was just after Edmund died, and I needed to get away."

"And?" Leo pressed.

"And nothing. I met her, had drinks with her, and that's it."

Leo shook his head. "There's something you're not telling me."

Drake's eyes roamed the suite before settling back on his brother. He didn't want to reveal how he'd come to know Cecily, but he needed to give Leo something to get him off his back.

"After dinner, I went to the hotel bar and there she was. I thought she was very attractive. We shared a few drinks, I invited her back to my suite, and..."

He left the rest unsaid, figuring his brother could use his imagination.

"That's a very romantic story, Drake," he said, sarcasm filling his voice. "And now you're getting married?"

"Now, I'm getting married."

Leo shook his head again. "Something's up. Either that, or you're a damn fool. Maybe I should get my answers from her."

He started to leave, but Drake grabbed him by the arm, stopping him.

"Let it go, Leo."

"I just want answers."

"I know what you're planning to do, and that's not what this family does anymore. If I say the matter is handled, then it's goddamned handled. Stay out of my business."

"It's not handled if we don't know who she is," Leo argued. "For all we know, she could be from a rival company sent in to fuck us over, and you just brought her into the family without a care."

"She's not," Drake said, simply.

"And you're so sure about that?"

"Yes, I'm sure. Leave her alone."

He tried to leave again, but Drake's grip on his arm tightened, and he moved in close to Leo's face and spoke in a low and menacing pitch.

"I said let it go."

Leo roughly shook his arm free of Drake's hold and then stared at him with disgust and pity. "I was right. You are a fool."

Drake felt his temper rise, but he took his own advice and let the insult wash over him. He turned to the mirror one last time, but while he straightened his tie, his gaze trailed over to his younger brother, and he made damn sure his eyes communicated that Leo was not to cross him.

"Fool or not, this is my first and only warning. Stay away from her."

CHAPTER TWO

*I*n the penthouse suite across the hall, Cecily sat at the vanity hastily applying her makeup. She'd learned the basics from some of the girls in the group home and later in college, but there hadn't been many occasions in her life that called for mascara and blush. She figured this counted as one of those occasions, even though she wasn't feeling especially joyful.

Her cell phone chimed beside her, and she paused in applying her lipstick to pick it up. She swiped at the screen and inwardly winced when she saw yet another text from Tony.

Tony: *I haven't heard from you, and I'm starting to worry. Call me now.*

She put the phone down and finished lining her lips, promising herself she'd call him later. She didn't like to worry him, but the only thing on her mind was getting through the day. Besides, if she called him now and told him what she was doing at this very moment, he'd blow a fuse and then try to talk her out of it. But she didn't want to be talked out of it. This marriage had to proceed without a hiccup. She was going to become the new Mrs. Morgan temporarily, find that money Edmund hid as well as the identity of his partner and then this would all be over.

She put the lipstick tube down and then turned and looked around the empty and quiet suite. Drake had his father and brother in his suite. Although they were no doubt attempting to talk him out of this, he at least had people in his corner. He had family with him.

Cecily never believed she'd ever get married, but on days when she let her mind daydream, she often wondered what that day would be like when she had no one to invite. There would be no one to help her into her dress, no one to do her makeup for her, no one to walk her down the aisle and no one to give her away. She had colleagues and some friends, but not anyone she would call family—not anymore. Life had stolen that away from her more than once that she would never try again to create a family for herself.

A knock on the suite door sounded, disturbing her self-pity.

"Come in," she called.

The doors opened and Gianna Morgan stepped in, looking beautiful in a beige, satin, one-shoulder dress with heels to match. Her long, brunette hair was slightly curled and clipped to one side, and her skin looked flawless. If Cecily wasn't the one wearing a white strapless, floor-length gown, she would've sworn Gianna was the bride. She looked to be Drake's type.

His first wife, Jasmine also looked like his type—glamorous, stylish and sophisticated. It didn't take more than a Google search to find information about her and the spectacular wedding they had. Hundreds of guests flew to Lake Como in Italy to watch the billionaire bachelor and his bride exchange vows. It was a royal affair. Unlike today, he hadn't married her in secret and their arrangement hadn't been strictly business.

"I thought I'd come and see if you needed any help," Gianna said.

"Thank you, but I don't think so," Cecily said, as she stood. "I think I'm ready."

She was about to move past her, but something in Gianna's eyes stopped her.

"Is something wrong?"

Gianna hesitated and then gave a weak smile. "My mother and I weren't very close. After my father died, she ignored me, but spoiled my brother. He became an addict, eventually went to prison, and she died still defending him."

"I'm sorry to hear that," Cecily said.

"The point is when I married Edmund, the Morgans became my family. I may not know why you and Drake decided to suddenly marry, but you're marrying into this family, too."

"Gianna—"

"And I won't stand by and let anyone hurt him. I'm sure you know about Jasmine, Drake's ex-wife," she said, as if reading Cecily's thoughts.

"I've heard about her."

"She did a number on him, and I won't let that happen again."

Cecily's back stiffened, but rather than take offense to the veiled threat, she realized she needed to take this opportunity to begin forming alliances with the Morgans. After all, the point in marrying Drake was to get close to his family.

"You don't need to worry," Cecily said. "I can promise you, I'm not here to hurt, Drake."

She just wanted that account and all of its embezzled millions.

* * *

Cecily walked down the aisle of the nearly empty church and thought of what she was doing. Growing up in a group home, she made the habit of keeping to herself and only interacting with a few boys and girls she'd come to trust. But most of the time, she was a loner and carried that same trait into adulthood. She wasn't the kind of woman used to receiving a lot of attention. So having to walk down the aisle of this church alone and having all eyes on her was making her anxiety go into overdrive.

If it wasn't for that offshore account, she would have scrapped this idea the moment it popped into her head. But this wasn't just for her—it was for Tony. They both needed to find that account and whoever shared it with Edmund. Once he died, whoever he or she was had inherited millions—stolen millions, and Cecily was going to find it. But her first step was to marry Drake Morgan.

She raised her head, put one foot in front of the other and started down the aisle. As she moved toward the front of the church, her eyes slowly moved about the room. Her gaze first fell on the patriarch of the family—Ivan Morgan. He was a formidable presence, even in the winter of his life. He was once a titan of the business world, and that spirit and commanding presence still radiated from him. Despite his retirement from Morgan Global Solutions, the fire of his ruthlessness still flickered within him, reminding everyone of his wealth and power.

Sitting beside him was Leo Morgan, the youngest son, glaring at her with outright suspicion. Cecily didn't take it personally because according to her research, Leo was fiercely loyal and protective of his family. Although he had a youthful innocence about him, it was overshadowed by his steely gaze, his hunger for power, and his unwillingness to let the shadows of his family's past go.

Gianna Morgan, Edmund's widow, sat in the same pew looking elegant and distinguished. Cecily read that she'd grown up in a small town just outside of Bakersfield and right after high school, she'd made her way north to San Francisco. She and Edmund met at a party, and the rest, as they say, is history. Judging from their brief encounter in the penthouse suite, Cecily concluded she was also the unofficial protector of the Morgan family, Ivan Morgan in particular. What was her marriage to Edmund like, and would he have entrusted her with the tens of millions he hid in an offshore account?

Lastly, her eyes fixed on the enigmatic Drake Morgan who stood solidly at the altar with his lean, athletic build and subtle handsomeness that drew her in without even trying. His eyes tracked her every move down the aisle and didn't look away, even when she was standing before him. She wanted to know what he was thinking, but it was likely he was regretting ever agreeing to this in the first place. She knew he wasn't keen on this idea of hers at all, but he had no choice. He'd entered into this arrangement long before today, and he was going to see it through until she was ready to end things. They were partners in this web of deceit and would stay partners until she was done with him.

He opened the doors to his suite and allowed her to precede him inside. She stepped over the threshold and looked around at the beautiful, opulent surroundings. It was a vast living area with a private bar, complete with floor-to-ceiling windows providing a spectacular view of downtown Houston. She looked to her right and through the double doors was a California king-sized bed that looked so soft and inviting.

"Can I fix you a drink?" He asked, coming up behind her.

She whirled around. "No, thank you. In fact, I should go. I only came to make sure you and I still had a deal."

"You did that already," he said. "Business is over."

He lightly brushed the backs of his knuckles down her bare arm, and she stepped away, escaping the feel of his touch.

"I shouldn't be here. This was a—"

Her words froze in her throat as he backed her up against the closed doors of the suite, pushed her arms up over her head and planted kisses along the curve of her neck. He brought his lips to her ears, and the warmth of his breath made her shiver with anticipation.

"Don't say this was a mistake. I've been wanting to touch you the moment you interrupted my lunch months ago."

"We have to get back," she said.

"It can wait," he insisted. "It's a shitshow going on in San Francisco. I have the PR team, the board, and my family calling me nonstop."

"It's time for you to take over," she said, peering into the depths of his eyes.

"I will lead, and I will get you that account—just not now." Still keeping her trapped, he used one knee to nudge her legs apart and fit himself perfectly between them. She felt the hardness between his legs and held her breath.

"Right now, for tonight, I just want to escape, and I want to escape with you," he said, huskily. "Have you ever felt that way?"

"More than you know," she admitted without thinking.

"Then let's stop talking."

"We need to keep this professional." Her eyes pleaded with him to stop, but her body had other thoughts—more wicked thoughts.

Ignoring her, he kept one hand locking her wrists together and allowed the other hand to trail over the curves of her breasts, down to her abdomen, past her waist and lower until his hands were underneath her dress. His eyes never wandered from hers as he

*caressed the backs of his knuckles over the lace of her panties and
then used his fingers to slowly pull them to the side.*

*She closed her eyes and let out an involuntary moan when his
fingers made contact with that intimate part of her.*

"Cecily?"

*She slowly opened her eyes, turned on by the deep, rich timbre
of his voice saying her name.*

*"Tell me something," he said. "Do you want to be professional,
or do you want to be wet?"*

"Cecily?"

In a flash, the memory disappeared, and she saw that the
minister was looking at her curiously.

"I'm sorry. What did you say?"

"I need you to repeat your vows after me."

"Oh. Of course." She looked to Drake who was also
regarding her curiously, but with a hint of something that
told her he knew exactly what she was remembering.

She tossed away thoughts of his hands and lips all over
her and recited the vows with no emotion and no commit-
ment to what they symbolized. Once this charade was over,
she needed to get to work.

"By the power vested in me and the State of California, I
now pronounce you husband and wife." The minister paused
and looked to Drake. "You may kiss your bride."

he wedding reception was an uneventful, quiet affair that took place in the Morgan family's estate in a private enclave of exclusive Presidio Heights. Cecily had only seen the place in pictures from drone shots. It was massive in photographs, but in reality, it was overwhelming. She couldn't imagine calling this place her home for the next six months.

It was early evening by the time the parade of cars pulled into the circular driveway lined with perfectly manicured trees. Cecily stepped out of the sleek black town car she'd shared with Drake and looked up at the imposing wrought iron gates that marked the entrance to the 20,000 square foot mansion. As she walked up the front steps, she was greeted by the imposing neoclassical facade with its grand columns and intricate details. It was a magnificent home, but it inspired no warmth or attachment within her. She hesitated before turning the ornate handle of the towering front door, bracing herself to continue her performance as Drake's new bride.

"Are you all right?"

She turned and saw Drake eyeing her. Behind him, Leo waited impatiently while Gianna walked hand in hand with Ivan up the entryway to join them.

"I think she's waiting for you to carry her over the threshold," Leo smirked.

Drake turned and gave his brother a look that told him to go to hell. He then leaned past Cecily, opened the door and gestured for her to go inside.

Stepping into the foyer, Cecily was instantly surrounded by opulent marble, priceless artwork, and a dazzling chandelier. As the rest of the family moved around her to get settled, Gianna offered to give her a tour. But she declined, promising they could do it another day. The truth was, Cecily was suddenly feeling in over her head. She was married to a billionaire. She was in his home, and none of her intentions were genuine. What she really needed was to find a quiet corner where she could get her head to stop spinning. But that would also have to wait as the staff was ushering everyone into the dining room for a celebratory feast.

The 12-foot-long dark mahogany dinner table was set with fine bone China plates, crystal glasses, and silverware fit for a festive occasion. Cecily sat directly across from Drake, trying not to make direct eye contact with him. Gianna sat beside Cecily, Leo sat next to his brother, and Ivan, ever the patriarch, sat at the head of the table. The meal of Wagyu beef fillet mignon with truffle mashed potatoes and asparagus tips was delicious. The mood around the table, however, was tense and somber.

"It was a beautiful ceremony," Gianna said, breaking the silence.

"Yes, it was," Ivan agreed. "It reminded me of when I married Maria. It was a small chapel, and only our closest friends and family came. Those are the marriages that last."

"Dad," Drake admonished while cutting into his slice of meat.

"What?" Ivan asked. "What did I say?"

"Dad's right," Gianna said. "I often wished Edmund and I had a small ceremony. He was the one who wanted a big to-do. We had nearly five thousand guests, and it made me a nervous wreck having all those people staring at me."

She turned to Cecily. "You're very lucky Drake honored your wishes."

"I chose to have it small to keep the media away," Drake said.

"Why?" Leo asked. "Why shouldn't the world meet your new bride?"

Cecily watched as Drake gave his brother a look that carried a subtle warning behind it.

Leo raised his hands in surrender. "Fine, but as beautiful as this day was, I have somewhere to be. Forgive me for not staying the night to celebrate your union, but make sure to save some cake for me."

"Where do you need to be at this hour?" Ivan asked, glancing at his watch.

"I set up a late dinner meeting with a client."

"What client?" Drake asked.

"I'll let you know if it pans out," Leo said. "Congratulations, brother."

He stood and then turned to Cecily. "Welcome to the family."

"Thank you," she said, not missing the sarcasm in his words.

Leo gave a mock bow and then left the dining room.

Ivan cleared his throat. "Since my nurse has me on a strict diet, you all will have to enjoy the cake without me." He stood from the table with Gianna's help. "Now, if you'll excuse me, there's been enough excitement for me today. I'm going to turn in."

He paused and divided a look between Drake and Cecily. "I wish you both the best of everything."

Drake nodded and Cecily didn't know what to say as she watched him leave the dining room and head to another wing of the house toward his first-floor suite.

Gianna faced them both and smiled awkwardly. "I know it looks like everyone is abandoning you two, but I really do have some friends to meet."

Drake chuckled. "It's all right, Gianna. You can go."

"Enjoy the evening and congratulations."

"Thank you," Cecily said.

She sat with Drake as she listened to Gianna's heeled steps along the tiled floor as she went upstairs to change. After a few moments, she chanced a look at Drake and started to speak but was then interrupted when Ilsa, the confectionary chef, entered the dining room carrying a double layer chocolate confection.

"Congratulations, Mr. and Mrs. Morgan," she said and then looked around the table with a frown. "Where is everyone?"

"Dad had to turn in and Leo and Gianna had plans," Drake explained.

She shook her head and then shrugged, placing the cake between them. "Oh well. More for the two of you to share."

"This looks delicious," Cecily said. "Chocolate cake is my favorite."

"Yes. Mr. Drake told me," Ilsa said, slicing a piece for both of them. She handed a plate to Cecily, but Drake silently refused with a wave of his hand and instead cradled his glass of wine. When they were once again alone, Cecily looked at him.

"How did you know?"

"You ordered it from room service that night in Houston after we fucked."

Her hackles instantly rose. She'd known him for just over a year, but that was long enough to know that he only said that to get a reaction out of her. But she wouldn't give him one.

"Oh. I'd forgotten," she said.

"I didn't."

They engaged in a staring contest in which Cecily was the first to look away.

"Your family all seem close," she said, taking a fork and slicing a small piece of the moist cake. "For people with money, you're lucky."

"Why didn't you invite anyone to the wedding?"

She shrugged, chewing the small bite of cake and resisting the urge to moan from the taste of its sweet richness.

"What would be the point? We both know this isn't real."

"My family was there."

"Like I said, you're very lucky."

"You didn't invite anyone because there's no one to invite."

Her eyes narrowed. "What are you talking about?"

He leaned back in the dining chair to study her. "Cecily Amelia Reed. Born October 17, 1985, in Show Low, Arizona to Joseph and Fatima Reed. They were killed in a car accident when you were ten. You have no other family, so you became a ward of the State."

"Haven't you been busy," she said, dryly.

"As a foster child, you maintained a 4.0 GPA throughout junior high and high school and when you graduated, you joined the Air Force. You did four years and upon leaving the military, used your GI bill to attend Northern Arizona University where you got your bachelor's in accounting.

Apparently, you enjoyed the work and returned for a masters and doctorate in accounting with a specialty in forensic accounting."

"That's all?" She asked.

"Anything I left out?"

"Why are you investigating me?"

He shrugged. "It seemed fair. Anyway, with all that stellar education, you could've been a CFO or even started your own firm. Instead, you'd rather shoplift a billionaire husband."

She put her fork down. "You know why we're doing this."

"Yeah, I do, but it doesn't mean I shouldn't find out exactly who the hell I married."

He downed the rest of his drink and stood. "I think I've played the groom long enough. I have somewhere I need to be. When you're ready, one of the staff will show you to your room."

"*My* room," she clarified.

"That's right," he said, and a slow, sly smile creased his lips. "This place is big enough. You don't need to sleep with me."

She was grateful her complexion didn't allow him to see her blush. "I wasn't suggesting—"

"Goodnight," he said and left the dining room.

She held her breath and waited, listening to his steps fade away. When she heard the front door open and then shut, she let it out. For a few more minutes, she sat alone at the dinner table, savoring the delicious cake and trying to ignore the emptiness of the room around her. She then put the fork down and absently fidgeted with her wedding ring which was an enormous diamond that felt heavy on her slender finger and a stark reminder that this union was just a business arrangement—not a love match.

ony was sprawled on the dingy couch watching an old Perry Mason rerun. He wasn't really watching the show, but instead had the TV turned on for the white noise—a distraction from his thoughts.

Where the hell was Cecily and why wouldn't she return his calls and texts? This entire plan depended on her, and if something happened to her, he would be all out of options.

The sudden chime of his cell phone startled him, but he practically leaped up and snatched it off the coffee table before swiping the screen to answer the call.

"Cee? Cee, where are you?"

"No, it's not *Cee*," the caller said, derisively speaking the nickname.

Tony winced, instantly recognizing the voice. "What's going on? I've been calling and texting her. Is she all right?"

"She's fine, and she hasn't returned your calls because she's been too busy getting married."

Tony pressed the phone to his ear and sat back against the sofa, stunned.

"Married? Married to who?"

"Who do you think?"

He took a moment to ponder and when the obvious answer came to him, his mind refused to believe it.

"Why would she do that?"

"Don't the two of you have a history? You know her better than I do, so you tell me why she'd marry Drake. What the hell is she up to?"

"I—I don't know."

"That's not the answer I'm looking for, Tony."

"Look, whatever she's planning, Cecily knows what she's doing. We can trust her."

"Maybe you can trust her, but I'm not so sure."

Tony straightened his back. He didn't like his decisions questioned.

"I don't have access to the financials, and you don't have the skills needed to find that account. Cecily has both. We need her."

A grunt sounded on the other end, and Tony assumed his words were getting through.

"I'll get her to meet me as soon as I can and find out where her head is at," he continued. "The goal is the account. Once we get that, this all ends."

Without a word, the other end disconnected. Tony tossed his cell back onto the coffee table and leaned forward to rest his head in his hands. Not only didn't he like his decisions being questioned, but he especially didn't like it when the people he was working with chose to stray from the plan. The moment he saw Cecily, he was going to remind her of that.

CHAPTER FIVE

It was her dress he couldn't stop thinking about. It wasn't a one-of-a-kind couture gown designed by some world-famous designer. It was a simple strapless number he assumed she'd bought at some boutique store, but it accentuated her curves in a way that was enough to bring him to his knees. Her brown skin seemed to glow against the white satin, and it took all of his strength not to touch her exposed shoulders with his hands or his mouth.

The other moment he couldn't get off his mind was the kiss. It was chaste, but the instant he touched her lips—God! They were full and moist, just like he remembered, and he'd been tempted to pull her further into his arms and deepen the kiss. He'd wanted the moment to last, but it was the claps from his family that snapped him back to reality and forced him to pull away from her.

Drake sat in the VIP section of Nova—the club he owned. He and his brothers often held private meetings and entertainment for their guests in the VIP area. But tonight, it was just him, alone with his frustrations.

The dim lighting cast a soft glow on the expensive

furnishings and the elite crowd below. He took a sip of his scotch, feeling the smooth burn of the alcohol as it flowed down his throat. His gaze scanned the room, taking in the pulsing beat of the music and the energy of the dancers on the floor. But despite the lively atmosphere, Drake couldn't shake thoughts of Cecily from his mind.

Just over a year ago, when they first met, he'd been instantly fascinated by her. She was intelligent and ambitious, and he had been drawn to her icy yet confident demeanor. But now, she was his wife, and for the sake of his sanity he needed to see her as nothing more than his business partner.

Just as he was comfortably lost in his thoughts, he noticed a familiar face making her way towards him. It was Elise, an old fling who had been in and out of his life for years. She had a furious look on her face, and he guessed she had found out about his marriage. He motioned for the security team to let her through.

"You're married?" She asked standing before him and shaking with incredulity.

"Sit down," he said calmly. "Let me get you a drink."

He poured her a glass and went to hand it to her, but she slapped it out of his hand in anger, causing the glass to crash to the floor with shards, ice and liquid spilling everywhere. His security team, as always on high alert, moved in.

"How dare you?" She asked, ignoring the men closing in on her.

Drake waved them away and then spoke in a tone now dangerous. "Either relax or get escorted out of here."

She must have seen the green in his eyes harden, because she took a few breaths and visibly calmed herself. Finally, she took a seat beside him, and for a moment they shared the silence while looking out at the dancers gyrating on the floor to the upbeat music. One of the servers came by and quickly cleaned up the mess.

Once she was gone, Elise spoke again. "What the hell is happening? I didn't even know you were dating."

"It's not what you think."

She turned to him, her eyes flashing and then dug in her clutch for her cell. She swiped through the pictures in her social media app and then put the phone close to his face.

"You're telling me this isn't what I think it is?" She asked in anger.

Drake barely glanced at the image on her phone. He knew it was a photo taken that afternoon just minutes after he and Cecily said their vows and kissed each other to seal the deal. When Gianna snapped the picture with her phone, he knew it was going to come back to bite him. He was a wealthy bachelor who was once again trying his luck at marriage, only this time with an unknown woman. The photo had spread like wildfire and eventually made its way to Elise. It was the main reason he'd left Cecily alone tonight. He didn't just need to get away from her and the carnal thoughts she conjured up—he had to do damage control.

"You told me you never wanted to get married again after that fiasco with Jasmine. Now, here you are with another damn ring on your finger." She pulled up his hand and then shoved it away. "You're married again, Drake—but not to me."

"This is different. This is business, and once our business is over, so is our marriage. Do you think I'd be sitting here on my wedding night if I was in love with her?"

"What kind of business?"

He shook his head. "That's between me and her."

"But you don't love her."

"No."

I'm just wildly attracted to her, he thought to himself.

For several moments, Elise glared at him, unwilling to let her anger go. Then, finally, she seemed to come to a decision. She sidled closer to him on the plush couch and ran her manicured fingers along his forearm. She then leaned in and whispered into his ear with a seductive voice that any other time would have set him on fire.

"Then come home with me."

He considered the invitation and then slowly shook his head.

"Thanks for the offer, but I should at least give the appearance that I'm a happily married man."

He clutched her hand and gently removed it from his arm. Then to save her pride from being injured, he leaned over and planted a small kiss on her cheek. With that, he rose, left her in VIP and left the club. Spending the night with Elise would be just the thing to remind him that this deal with Cecily meant nothing. It would all be over once she got what she wanted.

But fake marriage or not, the one thing his father grilled into his sons was loyalty. As long as Cecily was his wife, he wouldn't entertain another woman. But it wasn't just loyalty keeping him from Elise's bed tonight. His mind still couldn't rid thoughts of how sexy his bride looked in her simple, white dress.

CHAPTER SIX

ecily opened and rubbed her eyes to the sunlight creeping through the drapes. She turned on her back and stretched in the soft bed that was big enough for four people. Sitting up, she looked around the room and noticed in the light of day that it was the size of her condo, complete with a private balcony. Without warning, her thoughts went to Drake, particularly where he slept and how big his bed was. She then immediately tossed those thoughts aside, got up and showered in the en suite bathroom and dressed.

She made her way down the grand staircase, feeling the weight of the previous day's events heavy on her mind. Yesterday had been a whirlwind of activity and emotion, but today it was time to get to work. She couldn't deny that the thought of being in a home where everyone regarded her as a stranger was starting to take its toll on her nerves. But she had to remind herself that this was necessary if she was going to finish what she started. Drake and his family would just have to be uncomfortable until she got what she needed.

At the foot of the staircase, she looked to the right and

paused. She'd refused a tour of the home yesterday, telling herself she wasn't here to ooh and ahh over the Morgans' display of wealth. However, she was rethinking that as she couldn't help but admire the way the sun cast its morning rays into the conservatory.

It seemed to be a room tucked away within the mansion like a hidden gem with its lush greenery and soaring glass walls. Plants and delicate vines adorned every corner, their leaves reaching towards the sunlight, creating a natural haven.

At the heart of the room, standing alone and almost regally, was a grand piano. Cecily stepped forward and ran her hands along the black polished wooden frame. Her fingers didn't pick up dust, and she assumed that was thanks to the house staff. Sunbeams filtered through the foliage, casting dappled shadows upon the keys. It was an old piano, weathered by time, but it appeared to occupy a place of honor within the conservatory.

"Your breakfast will get cold."

She snatched her hand away from the piano and whirled around to find Drake staring at her with a look in his eyes that said he wasn't too happy to find her there. He was dressed impeccably in a navy suit and stark white dress shirt that was open at the collar.

"Sorry," she said, though not exactly sure why she was apologizing. "I didn't notice this room last night. But now, with all this natural light, it's…beautiful."

He didn't say a word.

"Whose piano is this?"

He hesitated and then expelled a slow breath before answering. "It belonged to my mother."

She'd researched the Morgan's enough to know that Maria Morgan succumbed to ovarian cancer four years prior.

"Was she the only one who played it?"

He extended his arm toward the door of the conservatory. "The rest of the family is waiting. Come eat."

His stare brooked no room for argument, so she put aside her curiosity for the moment and stepped past him out of the room. She remembered where the dining room was, but even if she didn't, all she had to do was let her nose lead her to the mouth-watering aromas of breakfast.

Her stomach rumbled from hunger. Because of her nerves, she'd barely touched her dinner last night and had only two forkfuls of the moist chocolate cake.

But the moment she entered the dining room, she could feel the tension in the air.

"Good morning," she said and received a chorus of greetings from the Morgan family ranging from cheery to disinterest.

Drake, who'd been trailing behind, moved past her and pulled out the same chair she'd sat in last night. The act of chivalry that came from such a brooding man, both surprised and intrigued her.

"Thank you," she mumbled, taking her seat.

"Did you sleep well," Ivan asked, salting and peppering his egg white omelet.

"Yes, I did," she lied.

Drake took his seat opposite her, poured himself coffee and then looked to his brother.

"How did that client meeting go?" He asked.

"I closed the deal," Leo said, beaming.

Drake nodded with a subtle smile. "Congratulations."

"I took them to Nova last night to celebrate," Leo said and then paused to frown. "Come to think of it, didn't I see you there in VIP with Elise? She's looking good these days."

Drake's smile slowly morphed into malice. Cecily looked up from her plate and caught his eye. The look between them was fleeting, but so many thoughts were racing through her mind, and she would give anything to know what he was thinking about, too.

He ignored the quip about Elise and continued to address Leo. "Have your assistant send me the details on the deal."

Leo chewed a bite of toast. "Will do, but I'm going to need you to trust me on this one, big brother. I know what I'm doing."

"I get final say," Drake said.

Leo regarded him, but Cecily could see his jaw hardening from slow-building anger. "That's fair."

Silence reigned around the table once again before Drake finally looked at his watch and got up from the table. "Have it on my desk within the hour."

"You're going into the office today?" Gianna asked, her voice filled with surprise.

"Yeah. Why not?" Drake replied, shrugging his shoulders.

"Well, you just—I mean, yesterday—," Gianna stammered, dividing an awkward look between him and Cecily.

"What Gianna is trying to say is you got married yesterday," Ivan said. "Shouldn't you be spending the day with your new bride?"

Drake barely looked Cecily's way as he answered. "It's just another day."

"Well, if you're going in, I'd like a meeting with you to go over the latest plans for Fuego," Gianna said, eagerly.

Drake nodded. "Call Tara to set it up. Let her know she can move things around so that it happens today."

With that, he turned and left the dining room. Cecily quickly excused herself, rose from the table and went after him.

"Do you have a minute?" She asked, catching up to him in the foyer.

"No, I'm late as it is," Drake answered as he shrugged on

his coat.

"I'll be quick."

He turned to look at her with impatience. Without his family's prying eyes, she was tempted to ask him about his visit to the club last night and the woman named Elise. But she didn't want to give him the satisfaction of knowing she gave a damn.

"I'll be in the office later today to start my search for that account," she said, careful to keep her voice down.

"Today won't work," he argued.

She narrowed her eyes. "Make it work. I'll also need an office to work out of temporarily. It doesn't have to be anything fancy, just someplace quiet. Get me access to the files, and I'll take it from there."

She started to turn away, but he gripped her elbow and swung her back around. "Can't you do this after hours? How am I supposed to explain to my assistant or anyone else why you're there or what the hell you're doing?"

Cecily immediately shook herself from his grasp. "That's not my problem. Just make sure I have access so I can get to work. I want that account, Drake. The sooner I find it, the sooner I'm gone."

She could see his irritation somewhat diminish and knew that if she kept dangling that carrot in front of him, he'd agree to almost anything.

"I'll text you the number to my assistant. Call her and tell her what you need," he said, already pulling out his phone. "I'll let her know to expect your call."

He turned and wrenched open the front door, revealing his irritation with her and their circumstances. She held the door open and watched as he climbed into the back seat of the waiting car. She couldn't see him through the dark tinted windows, but something told her he was eyeing her with just as much disdain as she was eyeing him.

CHAPTER SEVEN

"I have to say, I'm very impressed you stayed under budget for this project," Drake said, flipping through the typed report Gianna gave him.

Before she married Edmund, Gianna had been a high-end event planner. After her marriage, she'd put her career on hold to focus on being his attentive wife. After Edmund's death, she'd come to Drake asking him to put her to work, and he didn't hesitate to hire her to oversee and manage the opening of his new restaurant, Fuego, located in a trendy district of San Francisco.

"Well, you have to remember that one of the reasons Edmund married me was for my saving and investing skills. He was the spender between us," she said.

"I remember," he said. "Edmund definitely loved to spend money. So, where are we?"

"I'm finalizing the menu with the head chef tomorrow, and the décor is set to arrive this weekend. We're ahead of schedule."

"And I'm one day closer to seeing my new investment," he said, closing the folder and handing it across the desk to her.

"Absolutely. And make sure you bring your new wife to the opening and show her off to society."

He snorted. "That's not the kind of marriage Cecily and I have."

Gianna quirked an eyebrow. "Then what kind is it?"

Drake shrugged. "It's complicated."

She studied him for just a moment. "Leo and Ivan said you're being secretive about her, and that's your business. But we don't know anything about Cecily except for the fact that you insisted on marrying her, especially after you swore off marriage after your and Jasmine's very bitter and very public divorce."

"She's nothing like Jasmine. She's not here for money."

"Then what is she here for?" Gianna asked. "And don't tell me love because that's not it either. Don't get me wrong, there's definitely a spark between you two, but it's more attraction and lust—not love."

Heat rose up the back of his neck. "You're telling me you and Edmund were the perfect picture of matrimony?"

She looked taken aback, but instead of lashing back at him, she stood and gathered her purse and folio.

Drake also stood and reached across his desk to gently grasp her wrist and stop her from walking out.

"Gianna, I'm sorry."

"That was cruel," she said.

"You're right, and again, I'm sorry. Can you sit back down? There's something about Edmund I've been meaning to ask you."

She hesitated.

"Please."

She slowly sat back down, but her beautiful and exotic features were still guarded. "What is it?"

He pondered his words. "The last time you saw him— how was he?"

"What do you mean?"

"I mean how was his mood? Was he angry or worried?"

She shrugged. "He seemed like his usual self. I could tell there was something weighing on his mind, but you know Edmund. He was never the type to open up. He kept things bottled inside and only talked when he wanted you to know something. Why do you ask?"

Drake stared through her, watching the memory replay in his mind that took place in this very office, only this had been Edmund's office and Drake was sitting where Gianna was now sitting.

Drake felt uneasy about what was happening. He knew he had done the right thing, but he couldn't shake the feeling that he was betraying his brother. The room was filled with the sound of shuffling papers as Edmund gathered documents and stuffed them into his briefcase. The tension in the air was palpable, and Drake could feel it weighing heavily on him.

"There's something I need to tell you," Drake said.

Edmund's assistant entered the room, interrupting the uneasy silence. "Sir, the helicopter is on the roof waiting for you," she said, her voice crisp and professional.

"Thank you," Edmund said and then turned to Drake. "Look, whatever it is, it'll have to wait until I get back."

"Just give me a few minutes," Drake said, standing, but Edmund grabbed his briefcase and hurried past him.

"Drake, I know what you want to talk to me about," he said, his tone clipped.

"You do?"

"You don't think I know what you've been up to?"

Drake could see the rage behind his brother's eyes. "So, what now?"

"We'll deal with it when I get back. Right now, I have somewhere to be. While I'm gone, maybe you can decide where your loyalty lies."

Edmund moved past Drake, purposely nudging him in the shoulder. Drake turned and watched as his brother disappeared out of the door, feeling a sense of foreboding settle over him.

"Drake," Gianna said, snapping him out of the memory. "Are you all right?"

He nodded and stood to his feet to shake the past and his traitorous feelings away. "Let's pick this up another time. I have another meeting."

"Sure," she said, grabbing her oversized Chanel bag and rising to her feet. "It's good to see you in your element. If anyone is capable of turning things around after Edmund, it's you."

Drake nodded and walked her to the door. "Thanks for the vote of confidence."

He watched Gianna walk away, and when she was out of sight, he moved back to his desk and picked up his cell phone. Working under Edmund's leadership for years had made him distrustful. Edmund tried to hide his embezzlement from him, and he wasn't about to let his new wife pull the wool over his eyes either.

Last night, he'd ordered Cole to put a tracking device on Cecily's car. If she wasn't at the office, he wanted to know what she was up to. They may be working together, but he knew she was keeping him in the dark about other things. But he wouldn't be in the dark for long.

"Tara, push back all my meetings to this afternoon," he said, donning his jacket. "Call down to security and have my personal car waiting out front for me."

"You don't want me to call your driver?" Tara asked.

"No," he said. "Where I'm going, I need to be alone."

CHAPTER EIGHT

"Where the hell do you get off marrying him without talking to me first?" Tony asked in an undertone.

His body was rigid, and she could tell he wanted nothing more than to tear into her. Had it not been for the fact they were sitting at a corner bistro just off Market Street, she was certain he wouldn't be as restrained as he was now.

"It was necessary," she said. "With Edmund gone, I ran out of options. Marrying Drake gets me inside that house. It gets me access to his family and to his database without too many questions."

He frowned. "You think someone in the family was Edmund's partner?"

"It's just a hunch. Leo and Edmund were very close before he died. Leo looked up to him and wants to follow in his footsteps, and I sense a lot of resentment from him that Drake took Edmund's place as CEO."

She ran her fingers along the rim of her coffee cup, thinking. "There's also Edmund's wife, Gianna."

"I heard their marriage was rocky," Tony said. "You think he would actually give her access to the account?"

"Before Edmund died, Drake told me he overheard Edmund asking Gianna if her passport was up to date. It must not have been too rocky if he planned to take his wife out of the country with him."

Tony considered that but shook his head in disagreement.

"Yeah, but marriage, Cee? How in the hell did you get him to agree to that?"

"We made a deal," she said, keeping her voice calm and steady. "I have something he needs."

"And that is?"

"The skills to find the embezzler. Whoever was Edmund's partner isn't going to go away. My guess is they're still bleeding money from the company. Drake wants to find him or her just as much as I do."

Tony nodded, but the way he was looking at her told Cecily he believed she was in way over her head. There was also a subtle fury wanting to come out. His days as an Army Ranger squad leader got him used to making a plan and having it acted upon without the slightest deviation unless he was the one ordering the deviation. She'd acted alone, and to him, that was a cardinal sin.

On the other hand, Cecily wasn't used to answering to anyone, which is probably why their relationship ended so quickly.

Her expression hardened with determination. "I know you're upset I did this without your say so, but you need to trust me. I'm going to find that account and Edmund's partner. Once I do, I'll give you the credit and get your reputation back."

The steely gaze of his brown eyes softened a bit. "Why are you doing this? Why are you putting yourself on the line for me?"

She shrugged. "What happened to you wasn't right. They should've listened to you. Besides, we made a great team once. We weren't the best in a relationship, but everything else…it was good."

He looked around at the pedestrians passing by, taking advantage of the rare sunny morning when fog didn't envelop the sky and obscure the views. Letting go a heavy sigh, he then turned back to her and reached across the table and took her hand.

"I need you to keep me updated on this and to be careful. The Morgans, the sons especially, are very dangerous. Drake may be trying to turn the business around, but I've heard that he can be ruthless when he needs to be."

"I can handle Drake."

He clutched her hand tighter, and his touch made her think of the past before everything had grown complicated between them.

"I mean it. Find that money and then get the hell away from them." He paused. "And don't ghost me again. I still care about you, Cee."

She nodded, unsure how to take his words. After her parents died, there hadn't been many people who genuinely cared about her. There was the Atwood's, whose love she tried so hard to refuse. But in the end, she'd lost them, too, and she'd been refusing love ever since. Life was so much easier if she just kept her heart buried.

CHAPTER NINE

After saying goodbye to Tony and promising to meet him for periodic updates, Cecily left the bistro and made her way back to her car, while at the same time checking her messages. She listened to a voicemail from Tara, Drake's assistant, telling her that an office was ready for her as well as security credentials giving her access to the company's financials.

Cecily checked the time as she got into her car. It would be best if she drove straight to the offices of Morgan Global Solutions and began her search for Edmund's hidden offshore account, but her mind was frazzled after speaking with Tony. It always was when she was in his presence because being near him sent her traveling down memory lane and how things used to be between them.

For so long, she'd admired him as a colleague, which then turned into infatuation. Eventually, after months of subtle hints, he finally took notice of her, and they began to date. But it didn't take long for Cecily to realize that her feelings for him were much stronger than his were for her. She was constantly wanting to take things to the next level. It was the first time in her life, since losing her family, that she actually wanted to see how it felt to care about someone and possibly love them. But Tony seemed to be only interested in casual sex and nothing more. So, she ended things between them, but her feelings for him didn't turn off so easily.

When she pulled up to the old building on the other side of town, she parked, grabbed her supplies from the back seat and got out. As she always did, she took a moment to glance up at the decaying building and felt a visceral reaction of anger. These kids deserved a better building and better resources to display their gifts and talents.

You could do something about it.

The inner voice nagged at her and as always, she willed it to just shut up. Yes, she could do something, but it meant taking something that wasn't truly hers.

"Hey, Cee." Brandon, a young staff member greeted her as soon as she entered the lobby. "We haven't seen you in a while. We thought you forgot about us."

"Not a chance," she said, smiling. "I just had some personal stuff to handle. Any kids in the classroom?"

"Yeah, there's a few in there. They'll be excited to see you."

Cecily chatted with him a few more minutes before clutching her supplies and making the short trek down the hall. When she entered the room, the kids who'd been working in there alone turned and greeted her with excitement.

"I was in the mood to paint," she said. "Do you guys mind if I join you?"

They eagerly invited her in, and she moved to an open easel to set up her brushes and paint. This was the welcome distraction she needed to take her mind off her complicated feelings for Tony and her emerging yet unwanted feelings for Drake.

* * *

What was she up to?

Drake sat in his car a few cars down from Cecily and watched her go into the brick building. He'd followed her from Market Street where he watched her have coffee with a man at a bistro. The man had been unfamiliar to Drake, but the way he clutched Cecily's hand told him they were very close. He was glad when their little meeting had ended because he had the urge to walk up to them and break it all up. Now, she'd gone inside a building in a sketchy part of town with no signs on the outside revealing what kind of business it was—if it was a business. It reminded Drake of one of the establishments Edmund used to keep as a front to run illegal practices, meet with a shady investor, or punish someone who'd done him wrong.

Drake pulled out his cell and sent a quick text to Cole:

Drake: *I'm sending you a photo of a man Cecily was meeting with. Find out everything you can about him.*

Cole: *I'm on it.*

Drake: *Here's an address to a building in the Tenderloin. Find out what you can about this place, too.*

He input the address and sent off the text. In a few seconds, Cole texted back.

Cole: *Got it. I'll get back to you when I have something.*

Drake put the phone away and stared at the building a moment longer before turning his ignition and returning to the office for his scheduled meetings. He'll keep letting Cecily think she has the power, and the moment he got what he needed, he'd snatch it all away from her.

CHAPTER TEN

That evening, Leo stood at the threshold of the lounge watching his father and Gianna work on a puzzle together. The room was decorated with mahogany wood furnishings, and the walls were adorned with pictures of the family, Leo's grandfather and father being the prominent ones. Ivan sat at the card table, his gray hair slicked back and his piercing eyes concentrating on the pieces.

Ivan loved jigsaw puzzles. There were moments during his childhood where Leo remembered his father putting a puzzle together while at the same time finessing a merger. Yet, even with his love for something as innocent as puzzles, Ivan still managed to intimidate the hell out of Leo. He'd been dreading this meeting for weeks, knowing that it could end up being a heated argument.

"For Christ's sake, Leo, don't stand there at the door. Either come in or leave."

Leo nodded, his eyes fixed on his father as he took a seat in one of the club chairs and noticed a new painting on the wall. It was a serene landscape that seemed out of place in the otherwise formal surroundings, and he guessed it was an addition by Gianna. She was always adding her feminine touches throughout the mansion.

"Well, what is it?" Ivan asked, this time looking up at Leo.

"What I have to say is…private."

He sent a pointed look to Gianna. She nodded and began to rise.

"No," Ivan said reaching out a hand to forestall her. "You can stay. Besides, I have an idea what Leo wants to talk about, and if I'm right, this conversation won't last long anyway."

Leo rolled his eyes and decided to cut to the chase. "Dad, I have the experience, the drive, and the passion to lead Morgan Global Solutions into the future."

Ivan slowly leaned back in his chair, toying with a small puzzle piece.

"You have the drive and passion to run the company like Edmund did," he said, his voice cold. "But you also want to lead the way he did, ruthless and aggressive and with practices I won't stand for. That's not what this company needs right now."

Leo bristled at his father's words, feeling his anger already beginning to surge. He wanted to shout, to vent all the frustration and resentment he had been holding in for so long, but he knew that such emotion would only deafen his father's ears.

"I just want what's best for the company and for our family."

"So does Drake, and he's doing just fine as CEO," Ivan said.

Leo's eyes trailed over to Gianna who sat quietly across from Ivan, her eyes ping ponging back and forth between them. Leo couldn't place his finger on why, but he didn't trust her. He also didn't understand why his father kept her around after

Edmund's death, but he had a feeling Gianna had her hooks in him—just like she had her hooks in Edmund. Now, he was dead, and Gianna was alive reaping the benefits of being his widow.

Leo focused on her bare left ring finger and cursed inwardly. The very least she could do was honor her husband's memory by continuing to wear her wedding ring. Edmund hadn't been in the ground for more than a month before she chose to remove it.

"Listen, son, I understand how you feel," Ivan said, his voice softening slightly. "But Drake has proven himself. He's turned this company around, made it more ethical, more sustainable and definitely profitable. He's earned the right to be CEO."

Leo shook his head, feeling defeated. "You won't even give me a chance."

"You're getting your chance as COO," Ivan countered.

"I'm more than just a fucking COO," Leo exploded. "I know how the company needs to be ran!"

Ivan glared at him, and Leo saw that his outburst had done what he'd feared it would do. His father was done with this conversation. He put down the puzzle piece he'd been holding and rose to his tall, imposing height.

"The Morgan name is not just about power and dominance, Leo," he said with finality. "It's about honor and integrity. I thought I taught you boys that, but apparently, Edmund didn't get it, and I can see you don't, either. That's why you're not my CEO."

He stalked out of the lounge, leaving Leo to regret his impulsive actions. After several moments of tense silence, he looked to Gianna who was returning his stare with disapproval.

"You have something you want to say to me?" He asked. "Say it."

"Your father's right," she said. "Drake is what the company needs now."

"What do you know about this company?"

She stood from the table. "I know enough. I saw how Edmund ran things. I turned a blind eye to it, but I knew it couldn't go on like that under his leadership."

"Is that why you don't wear your wedding ring anymore," Leo asked, stepping into her personal space. "Because my brother wasn't a good leader?"

"No, I don't wear it anymore because your brother wasn't a good husband. Loyalty and faithfulness weren't his strongest traits."

Leo looked her up and down with a sneer. "You did all right for yourself."

"Yes, I did," she said, matching his look. "I was his wife during those dark days, and I won't apologize for being compensated for it."

"You don't know what you're talking about."

"I knew my husband, Leo, and you'll never be him," she said. "And I know you don't believe this, but that's actually a good thing."

She marched out and Leo watched her go, brimming with fury. When he was finally alone, he swiped the half-completed puzzle from the table and watched with satisfaction as hundreds of tiny pieces scattered to the floor.

CHAPTER ELEVEN

One year ago...

The midday sun beat down on the bustling streets of downtown San Francisco, casting long shadows along the crowded sidewalks.

Cecily sat in her car, hidden among the throng of vehicles, her gaze fixed on the entrance of the restaurant across the street. Behind the tinted windows, she peered through her binoculars, her heart pounding with anticipation. This was her chance to get close to Drake, the elusive younger brother of the CEO, Edmund Morgan.

Drake, the COO of Morgan Global Solutions, had always been surrounded by a wall of employees and associates. He seemed like an impenetrable fortress, but today, her patience had paid off. There he was, sitting at a table near the window, seemingly engrossed in his lunch and enjoying a rare moment of solitude.

Through the binoculars, she was able to observe him and study his features as much as she wanted. Her first thought was that he was undeniably handsome. His dark hair was perfectly styled, and the faded goatee framed a chiseled jawline that spoke of confidence and determination. But Cecily couldn't afford to let her thoughts dwell on Drake's attractiveness. Her mission was to get access to Edmund Morgan's stolen millions.

Taking a deep breath, she lowered the binoculars and got out of her car. She walked purposefully towards the restaurant, her strides confident and measured. Her sleek black suit blended effortlessly with the city backdrop, and the sound of her heels clicked against the pavement.

She entered the doors of the high-end restaurant, revealing a warm interior bathed in the golden hues of afternoon sunlight. The clinking of cutlery and the murmurs of conversation filled the air, creating the perfect ambiance for closing business deals or conducting covert meetings like hers.

Cecily's eyes darted across the room toward the window seats, scanning for Drake, and she spotted him in the corner, his gaze divided between his cell phone and medium rare steak.

Without hesitation, she strode toward the table, her heart pounding against her ribs. She could feel the weight of the photos in her pocket, evidence of the dark secrets going on within his company.

"Hello, Mr. Morgan," Cecily said, standing in front of his table.

Drake looked up with surprise etched across his face as she pulled out the chair across from him and sat down.

"I didn't give you permission to join me," he said, his voice husky with a tinge of danger. "If you want a meeting with me, call my assistant."

Ignoring his protests, she reached into her pocket, producing some black and white photos and laid them on the table in front of him. "I'll make this quick so you can get back to your lunch. Take a look at these."

Drake didn't move but continued to regard her with restrained hostility.

"Look at them," she ordered.

His eyes shifted downward, and he studied the photos. He picked up one photo and traced the images with his finger. Cecily watched his reaction carefully, silently analyzing every twitch and shift in his expression. She'd put before him various images of Edmund supervising beatings of rival clients, someone who owed him money, or anyone who dared to cross him. She watched Drake closely and saw the slightest flicker of recognition in his eyes—a glimmer of understanding that told his knowledge of his brother's dark deeds.

After a moment, she leaned forward, her gaze unwavering. "Not only is your brother committing these acts, but he's been stealing from the company your father built."

As Drake continued to study the photos, Cecily studied him. Being so close to him now, she could see the pictures of him hadn't done him justice. His face held a vulnerability, a conflict within his soul that drew her to him, but she ruthlessly shut it away and remained focused on what she came here to do.

"I need your help. You have a choice. You can choose to ignore what's happening, to turn a blind eye to your brother's actions, or you can protect your family's legacy."

She leaned back, her gaze never leaving his face. Drake's gaze slid from the photos to the window. He drummed his fingers on the table while staring outside at the street traffic. Finally, he seemed to conquer whatever silent war had been raging within him and slid the photos back to her.

"You know my name, but who are you?" He asked.

"Cecily Reed."

"Well, Cecily Reed, thank you for enlightening me, but let

me enjoy the rest of my lunch that you interrupted and don't ever contact me again."

She had to keep herself from exploding. She had underestimated the depth of his loyalty, even in the face of such damning evidence. But something told her she had gotten through to him, even if he refused to admit it outright. She gathered the pictures and tucked them away. Then she pulled out a pen and scribbled her number on the back of a piece of scrap paper from her pocket. She slid the paper to him, her eyes fixed on him and silently praying he didn't rip it up.

"I didn't think you wanted your family company known for these kinds of acts," she said. "When you're ready to help, call me."

With that, she stood from the white linen-covered table, turned away and headed for the exit, feeling the weight of Drake's gaze burning into her back as she left.

Damn. She hoped she didn't just screw things up with the only man who could get her access to the money.

CHAPTER TWELVE

Cecily stared at the computer monitor, trying to get the numbers to talk to her. Somewhere in there was a mystery, and she was going to solve it. Tony was counting on her, and the last thing she wanted to do was make him feel as though she weren't up to the job. Next to him, she was a brilliant forensic accountant. When money needed to be found, she was the one that was called—that is, if Tony wasn't available.

But Edmund had done a damn good job of burying the offshore account because it had been over a month, and this was proving to be her most difficult assignment to date. She'd only managed to find a shell account in Zurich and followed the trail to Athens and then Liberia where that account was a shell for another account, but that was as far as she'd gotten. Still, she could at least give this information to Tony and compare it to his own findings.

She downloaded all the information she'd found so far, transferred it from the company computer to her laptop and shut everything down. She then leaned back in her chair, stretched and looked around, realizing she was the only one left on the floor.

Checking her cell phone display, she saw it was ten minutes past eight. She put her laptop in her messenger bag, grabbed her coat and purse and took the elevator down to the lobby of the building. She said a polite goodnight to the security guard on detail and paused at the sight of rain pouring outside. Sighing, she reached inside her bag and pulled out her umbrella. She planned to take the BART to Potrero Hill to see Tony and hopefully, she wouldn't arrive too wet.

She walked a few blocks through the financial district on her way to the BART station, but as she came to the edge of the block, a black town car pulled to the curb, blocking her path to cross the street.

Cecily frowned, unable to see through the dark tinted windows of the town car, but in seconds, a tall, imposing man in a black suit stepped out of the driver's seat and rounded to the other side. She recognized him immediately as Drake's driver, Hank. When he opened the back door, Cecily leaned down and saw the man himself peering at her from inside.

"Good evening," he said, speaking loudly to be heard over the pouring rain. "Are you heading home?"

"You mean back to your mansion? Eventually, yes, but I have an errand to run first and then I'll catch an Uber back."

"I'll take you to run your errand and then you can ride back with me."

Cecily stood frozen, feeling a bit uneasy. She didn't want him to know about Tony and started to decline the offer.

"It's not a request," he said. "Get in."

Cecily looked to Hank, who was holding the door open for her. He, too, didn't look to be in the mood to argue with her, especially with the rainfall. She closed her umbrella and quickly got inside. The door closed after her, effectively trapping her inside the quiet darkness with Drake and his intimidating presence.

They'd been married just over a month now, and this was the first time she had a moment alone with him. It seemed they both were skilled at avoiding each other. Their bedrooms were on opposite sides of the hall, the office he set up for her was practically a utility closet set up on the same floor as his office, but in the opposite direction. Whenever he worked late, she came home early and vice versa, so they even managed to avoid having dinner together.

"I can run my errand later," she said. "Let's just head back to your place."

As soon as the car began to move, Drake reached over and snatched her messenger bag away from her. He then pulled the laptop out and wasted no time powering it on.

"What are you doing?" She asked in alarm.

"What's the password?" He demanded.

She was momentarily speechless, but it was out of curiosity that she gave him her password, and it didn't take long before he found the file with the documents she'd downloaded earlier. He started to read through them and Cecily frowned.

"Is there something I can help you with?"

"You didn't find the account," he guessed.

"Not yet. Just a shell account that led to a dead end."

"Then this information is useless."

Before she could stop him, he made quick work of deleting the files. Staring open-mouthed, Cecily watched as the documents vanished from her hard drive. He handed the laptop back to her, and she snatched it away, angrily shut it down, and put it back in her bag. She then turned in her seat to face him, fuming.

"I think you've grossly misunderstood our arrangement, so let me make this clear: I'm the expert here. Not you."

"Anything you find, you run it by me first," he said.

"Not if it compromises everything."

"The only way it would compromise anything is if I were directly involved."

Those words brought a silence in the car that was telling.

"Now, we're getting to the truth," he said as a knowing smile creased his lips. "Do you think I'm involved? Do you think I know where that account is?"

"I don't know. But this ambush doesn't convince me otherwise. You'd better not be holding out on me, or this arrangement is terminated."

The smile slowly disappeared as he gritted, "I don't take threats too well."

"And I don't take being played for a fool too well."

"As long as we understand each other," he said.

He moved so fast, she was once again powerless to react as he reached across the seat, gripped her by the arms and pulled her into him. His breath fanned her face as he got so close, she could see herself in the reflection of his green eyes.

"I gave you that office far away from me so that I wouldn't have to see you everyday and remind myself that I was deceiving my family."

"You're not deceiving them," she softly argued.

"They don't know who you are, and if I told them how you basically blackmailed your way into this marriage, how I betrayed Edmund..."

"It needed to be done. We've been going at this for too long."

She took hold of his arms now, but it was out of desperation. She couldn't let him back out now. She needed to finish this for Tony.

"Just a few more months, Drake. Let me find the money,

and then it's over. You can avoid me for another month if that helps."

"So, you noticed?" He asked and then shook his head. "I avoided you because even though I despise having you as my wife, I can't stop thinking about you and the one time you let me see a glimpse of the woman you really are."

She opened her mouth to speak because something in her wanted to be truthful with him, but something hidden deep within pressed her to stay quiet. She saw that the fury in his eyes had also quieted to a dull blaze. He slowly moved his gaze from her eyes down to her lips and stayed there as if he were studying their fullness and trying to remember their softness. She desperately wanted to remind him.

But it was as if something inside him snapped, jarring him back to his anger. He tore his eyes from her lips and instantly shoved her away from him.

The rest of the ride to the estate was filled with tension waiting to erupt like a dormant volcano. Cecily kept her head turned toward the window, afraid that if she looked his way again, she'd be forced to act on the buried desires he made her feel.

She released a pent-up breath when the car pulled to a stop, and she saw the palatial mansion through the pouring rain. But when they turned into the large circular driveway, she heard Drake emit a low but audible curse. She turned to him and then followed his angry gaze to a silver Mercedes SUV parked in front of the house. Cecily didn't recognize it as belonging to any member of the family.

"Are you expecting company?" She asked.

Hank pulled the car to a stop behind the Mercedes and Drake didn't wait for the door to be opened for him. Without answering her, he jumped out, slammed the back door and made long, forceful strides to the front door. Cecily thanked

Hank for opening her door and hurriedly followed after Drake.

As soon as she walked into the house, she drew up short when she saw him speaking in hushed tones to an attractive woman with fiery red hair and goddess-like features. Despite enduring tragedy and being orphaned at a young age, Cecily always prided herself on her high self-esteem and self-worth, but being in this woman's presence made her feel lacking.

Drake abruptly ended his hushed conversation the moment he noticed they had an audience. He met Cecily's eyes and became visibly uncomfortable, but it was nothing compared to the fury coming from his mysterious guest.

"Let's go in the study," he said to the woman.

He led her into the room just off the foyer and before closing the double doors, he sent Cecily a look that she couldn't quite decipher.

CHAPTER THIRTEEN

Gianna sat in the large lounge with Ivan and Leo. Ivan, as usual, was working on a jigsaw puzzle, Leo was scrolling through his phone, and Gianna was watching a video on her tablet. She very much enjoyed these quiet moments with the family just before dinner. They always brought her comfort, especially when Edmund used to work late hours. His family had become her family.

Soon, she heard heels marching along the marble floor. She looked up from her tablet just as Cecily appeared in the entry of the lounge. She looked around and mumbled "good evening" to everyone.

"Good evening, my dear," Ivan said. "Come sit with us for a bit. Dinner will be ready soon."

"Thank you," Cecily said, smiling.

Gianna's eyes trailed Cecily as she chose a seat in an over-sized armchair beside her. It wasn't the first time Gianna studied the woman who so suddenly and mysteriously became a part of their family. The moment Drake announced he was marrying her, Gianna made it her sole focus to find out everything she could about Cecily Reed. She had to admit there wasn't a lot to learn about her online—she had no social media accounts to speak of, and a simple background check only yielded the most basic information about her. The most compelling thing Gianna could come up with was that Cecily was educated in finance and she'd been an orphan. Her identity was so secretive that the wedding had been the first time Gianna ever laid eyes on her.

She had to admit the woman was stunning. Her dark brown skin was smooth and flawless. She wasn't super model thin, but her body was curved and statuesque, giving her the appearance of elegance when she walked into a room. Her hair, which she seemed to wear in its natural state, was full of bounce and no matter which way she turned, her curls always managed to frame her oval-shaped face. The only part of her that made Gianna feel uneasy were her eyes. They were dark brown, elusive, and full of mystery. She noticed them the day of the wedding when Gianna warned her not to hurt Drake. Cecily hadn't cowered in the least.

"Did my brother come home with you?" Leo asked, looking up from his phone.

Cecily, who had also pulled out her phone to scroll through it, looked up and nodded to Leo. "He's in the study."

At the mention of Drake, a shout was heard coming from the direction of the study. Cecily hadn't closed the doors to the lounge, and it was all too obvious that the shout was a woman's voice.

Leo chuckled. "It seems we might have another guest for dinner."

"Leo," Ivan said in a warning tone, as he fit another puzzle piece into the forming picture on the card table.

In response, Drake's voice could be heard as it matched the woman's anger. It wasn't often Gianna heard her brother-in-law become angry. Edmund had been the hothead of the family, a man quick to react in anger when he didn't get his way, and it seemed Leo was following after his oldest brother. But Drake was the one with the cool and calm demeanor, something a true leader should have. But ever since he'd brought his new wife home, Gianna had been seeing a different side of him.

The two voices in the study were now competing in decibel levels, and Gianna slyly slid her gaze over to Cecily. The woman was clutching her cell phone in her hand tighter; her shoulders were stiffer and her back straight. What could she be thinking hearing her husband arguing with another woman?

Ivan sighed. "Leo, close the doors, please."

"No," Cecily said, shooting up from her seat. "I'll take care of this, and I'll close the doors behind me. I'm sorry for the disturbance."

Gianna regarded her with surprise. She then turned to her father-in-law who looked uneasy at first but then nodded his head. Leo still wore a condescending smirk and couldn't resist getting a parting shot in as Cecily left the room.

"Ask your husband where he'd like us to seat his girl-friend at the dinner table."

Cecily regarded him with cold aloofness and then shut the double doors of the room behind her.

Gianna turned to Leo in disgust. "Do you have to be such a jerk?"

Leo sneered. "There's something fucked up about their whole arrangement. Business deal, my ass. I'll bet she black-mailed herself into the marriage for money, and if Drake had any damn balls, he would've gotten rid of her the second she became trouble."

"Stop it!" Ivan demanded. "I don't want to hear any more of that kind of talk. Those ways died with Edmund. Do you understand me?"

Leo looked as though he wanted to challenge his father, but he ultimately backed down.

"Sorry, Dad," he muttered and went back to scrolling through his phone.

Ivan returned to his puzzle, but Gianna could tell he was no longer relaxed. She tried to focus once again on the video she'd been watching, but it was impossible when what she really wanted to witness was the scene happening in the study at this very moment.

CHAPTER FOURTEEN

*D*rake closed the doors to the study, and stood there a few seconds, trying to keep his temper from exploding. But when he finally turned to confront Elise, he knew he hadn't done a good enough job of reigning in his fury because she took a slight step back.

"Don't ever show up here uninvited again," he warned.

"It's been a month, and I needed to see you," she said.

"You could've called. You could've met me at the club—not here at my house."

"Why not? I used to be welcome here."

"You know why."

"Because of your fake marriage?" She asked, her voice rising.

"Yes, exactly, and keep your voice down."

Elise stood before him, her eyes searching his for answers. The tension between them was thick and heavy like a dense fog that refused to dissipate. She was beautiful, with her long, red hair falling in soft waves around her face, and her eyes sparkling with a mixture of anger and hurt. He tried to be careful with his words, but the stress of the past year had been building up inside him and was threatening to boil over.

"How long is this supposed to go on?" She asked, her voice tight with emotion.

"That's between me and Cecily," he replied, his tone clipped and harsh.

"You and Cecily," she mocked. "It's been over a month already. How long am I supposed to wait for you?"

"I never expected you to wait for me," he said, clenching his fists. "We were never serious, Elise. You know that what you and I had together was just fun. You got to say you were dating an eligible bachelor, and I had a date to take to my events. I never led you on or promised any more than that, so spare me the victim act. I have more important things to worry about than an imaginary relationship you concocted."

She took a step forward, her hand raised as if to strike him. But he was quicker, catching her wrist in midair and holding it firmly. He could feel her struggling against his grip, her anger fueling her strength.

"You bastard," she hissed.

"Stop acting as if you're hurt," he said, his voice low and menacing. "I know how you feel about me. Find someone else to pose for your social media posts."

Elise snatched her hand away and marched out of the room. He followed closely behind her, and as soon as they exited the study, she drew up short. Drake came up behind her and saw that Cecily was standing in the foyer, watching them both. Elise looked Cecily up and down and for a moment, seemed transfixed on her necklace. She then turned back to Drake with eyes clouded with hurt and anger. Without another word, she continued to the front door, snatched it open and was gone.

Drake watched her stiff and angry march to her car. As soon as her Mercedes peeled away from the driveway, he closed the front door. He turned around, spared Cecily a momentary glance and then returned to the study. He headed to the small side bar to pour himself a drink and sensed her standing by the door watching him. Growing tired of the silence, he put the glass down with a thud.

"If you're waiting for an apology from me, you're wasting your time," he said.

"I never expected one," she said. "You were one of the city's most eligible bachelors. Frankly, I'm surprised there aren't more women parading through here and demanding an explanation."

"I only date one woman at a time," he said, and only because he didn't want to seem disrespectful, he added, "It won't happen again."

"Is she somebody special?"

"What do you care?" He asked. "What do you care who I love?"

He didn't know why he said that. He cared deeply for Elise, but what they had he wouldn't even begin to describe as love. But saying the words was worth it, because he noticed the slightest flash of anger in Cecily's eyes. Seeing that bit of chink in her armor pleased the hell out of him.

"I only came in here to tell you that dinner will be ready in a few minutes and that unless your guest was staying for dinner, maybe your conversation could continue somewhere else."

She started to leave, but Drake wasn't yet ready to let her escape. He stalked to the door and pulled her back inside just as she crossed the threshold. He turned her around, slammed the door and moved in close until her back was pressed against it.

"Answer the question," he demanded. "Why do you care who I love?"

"Number one: I don't care and number two: if you love her, then why am I in this house and not her?"

"Because I never intended to get married again. Like you said, I was a divorced, eligible bachelor, and I preferred to stay that way. I'm married to this company. Women are a pleasant distraction, a way to ease my stress. Nothing more."

Another flash in her eyes. God, he loved that he was breaking her defenses down. Any moment now, he would see all of her, not some ice queen, but the real, raw Cecily—like he saw in Houston that night.

"What is it?" He asked. "Do you want to know if that's what I think of you?"

"Get your hand off my arm," she said, coolly.

He moved his head to the side of her face, bringing his mouth close to her ear. "Do you want to know if that's what I thought of our night together?"

"I don't care what you thought of that night, and I'd prefer it if we'd forget it ever happened."

"I don't believe that." His mouth dipped lower to her neck where her exposed skin tempted him.

He could hear her breath quicken as he spoke in low, vibratory tones. "Just ask me, Cecily. Ask me what I thought of that night. Ask me what I thought of having you in my arms."

Her lips parted slightly, and her eyes closed. "I—I—"

"What?" He asked, his own breath quickening.

He wanted to touch her, to taste her, and it was pure agony. He'd gone a month avoiding her, but all it did was increase his need for her. If she would just give him the word, they could end this torture session, skip dinner, and be writhing naked in his bed in less than a minute.

"I don't care because I barely remember that night."

It was as if someone had tossed cold water into his face. He slammed an open palm against the door behind her, his fury erupting. He thought he had her, but in truth she had him the entire time. She'd been breaking him down.

"Liar," he gritted.

Cecily said nothing, but he could see the ice forming and once again, he was closed off to her. But those full lips of hers were still begging for him.

He leaned in, moving his gaze from her lips to her eyes and back again. It was the only place she didn't shut him out. She wanted the kiss just as much as he did.

A brisk knock sounded at the door, and Drake instinctively pulled Cecily away from it and moved to shield his body in front of her just before it swung open. Gianna appeared on the other side of the threshold, peering at the two of them curiously.

"I'm sorry to interrupt, but dinner's ready," she said.

Drake struggled to calm his breathing, but it was damn difficult when he could feel the rapid heartbeat of the woman standing so close behind him.

"Thank you, Gianna, we'll be right there."

"Actually, I'll come with you now." Cecily stepped from behind Drake and went to stand beside Gianna. "I didn't have much of a lunch, and I'm starving."

Gianna continued to divide a look between them as Cecily eased past her and headed for the dining room. When she was out of sight, Gianna turned her full attention on Drake with an inquisitive frown.

"Is everything all right?" She asked.

He raked a palm down the front of his face. "No, everything is not all right. I'm married."

ecily walked into the dining room, her heart racing as she relived the near kiss with Drake. She had to keep reminding herself why she was really here, and it wasn't to question Drake about his dating life. She should've just stayed in the lounge with the rest of the family, but something inside her pushed her to confront him. He'd spent their wedding night with Elise and even though that shouldn't have bothered her, they'd gone a month deliberately avoiding each other. The simple truth was, she'd missed him, and curiosity had her wondering if he was spending all of his free time with the illustrious Elise.

What was the matter with her? Who cares what the hell he did or who he did it with, as long as he stayed out of her way and let her find Edmund's millions.

As she took her seat at the dinner table, she tried to calm her nerves by focusing on her plate of food. But every time she lifted her fork to take a bite of the pan-fried fish fillet in brown butter sauce, she could feel Drake's eyes on her, making it difficult for her to enjoy the meal. She knew it was cruel of her to deny the memory of their night together in

Houston, but she couldn't allow thoughts of him and his touch to distract her from what she was supposed to be doing. She couldn't let her conflicting emotions get in the way of her and Tony's mission.

Ivan Morgan sat at the head of the table, regaling the family with tales from his days of running the company before he retired, but Cecily could barely pay attention. She glanced over at Leo, who was looking at her curiously. She quickly looked away and took a sip of her wine in the hopes it would calm her nerves.

"Are you packed for your trip to Vegas?" Ivan asked, turning to her.

"Vegas?" She put her glass down and dabbed at her mouth with a linen napkin. "What's happening in Vegas?"

Ivan raised an eyebrow. "Drake hasn't told you? He's overseeing the construction of a new hotel and casino in Vegas. I assumed he would take you with him."

Cecily glanced across the table at Drake, who was wearing an unreadable expression. She turned back to Ivan, trying to keep her voice steady. "No, I didn't know about the trip. But I have a lot of work to do here."

Drake cleared his throat. "I plan to go on my own, Dad. I have a lot to take care of and won't have time to entertain Cecily."

Ivan looked from Drake to Cecily and back again, a hint of confusion in his eyes.

"Well, maybe next time," he said finally.

"Just make sure you're back in time for the opening of the restaurant," Gianna said. "The whole family needs to be there."

Drake nodded and smiled. "I wouldn't miss it for the world."

Cecily turned to Gianna with a questioning frown and Gianna laughed.

"Oh, I'm sorry, Cecily. A lot of these events were already underway before you and Drake were married, and I can't believe he hasn't brought you up to date."

She paused to send Drake a scolding look and then returned her gaze to Cecily. "I've always wanted to manage a restaurant. I found this nice little place in a trendy, up and coming part of downtown. The owners were drowning in debt, and Drake made them an offer to buy it and hired me to rehab and manage it. For months, I've been working with contractors to revamp the place, and I have to say, I'm very proud of the work."

"We could use the investment," Drake said as a small, indulgent smile creased his lips.

But Cecily sensed it was something more. After Edmund's death, she guessed he was looking for a way to help his sister-in-law find her purpose and remind her she was still part of the family. Cecily grudgingly respected him for that.

"I can't wait to see it," Cecily said.

Ivan turned to Leo and sighed before sampling the caviar-infused risotto.

"Leo, you've been on that phone all evening. Is everything all right?"

Leo sent off another quick text and then put his phone down. "Sorry, Dad. It's just a few loose ends at work."

"Anything I need to know about?" Drake asked.

Leo raised his wine glass as a mocking salute to Drake. "It's just something to do with the Rosenthal deal. I've got it handled."

Cecily's ears pricked up. "What's the Rosenthal deal?"

"It's an old warehouse building we own on Rosenthal Avenue in Bayside. One of Edmund's purchases," Drake said.

He then turned to Leo. "I thought we unloaded that property months ago."

"Like you said, we needed the investment, and it's a good property. I made the decision to keep it. Even as COO, I still have some power," Leo added bitterly.

"But it's not just an investment," Drake challenged. "That place is a gambling den. From what I remember, there were at least seven more, and I told you when I took over that I wanted them all shut down."

Leo stayed quiet but watched Drake with cool defiance.

"I kept you on as COO because I thought I could trust you," Drake said. "What part of 'shut them down' don't you understand?"

"You *kept* me on as COO?" Leo asked with clarification. "No, I'm COO because it's my company just as much as it's yours."

Drake didn't back down. "You're entitled to a share in the profits, that's it. I don't have to employ you, and the fact that I have to clean up your mess tells me I made a big mistake."

"What are you two talking about? What gambling dens?" Ivan asked.

"They were dens Edmund set up to clean money from his illegal dealings, Dad. When I took over, I wanted them dismantled," Drake explained and then turned back to Leo and gritted. "We're not in that kind of business anymore. I'm turning this company around."

"They generate a massive amount of revenue," Leo said. "I thought we were in business to make money."

"We make plenty of money with the investments I set up," Drake said. "You damn well know that! We don't need to be involved in anything like that anymore. I made this clear from the word 'go,' and here you go behind my back defying every fucking word and assuming I wouldn't find out."

"You're making more out of this than necessary," Leo said, sounding bored.

Drake glared at his brother. "I'll say this one more time: Shut. Them. Down."

Cecily regarded the tense look between the two brothers and then took her linen napkin from her lap and put it on the table.

"I'm going to turn in early. Good night, everyone."

The moment she returned to her room, she powered on her laptop and accessed the files of Morgan Global Solutions remotely. It was only a matter of minutes before she found the file called *Rosenthal*. She opened it and just as Drake had said, it was a warehouse located in Bayside.

She made a mental note of it. If it had been one of Edmund's purchases, it may be an indirect link to his offshore account. She was chasing a long shot, but she was willing to try anything that would get her access to Edmund's partner and the hundreds of millions they were hiding.

CHAPTER SIXTEEN

One year ago…

Drake stood in Edmund's lavish office, his fists clenched tightly at his sides. The walls were adorned with expensive art pieces, and the large windows offered a stunning view of the city skyline. The office furniture was sleek and modern, with a large desk dominating the room. The plush carpet beneath Drake's feet was so soft he felt as though he were sinking into it. But the opulent surroundings were a stark contrast to the tension that filled the room.

"You need to resign," Drake said, his voice low with barely concealed anger.

Edmund looked up from his desk, his face contorted with fury. "I'm not leaving. This is my company, and I brought it to greater heights."

Drake shook his head in disbelief. "Our father built this company, Edmund. It's a family business, not yours to do whatever you please, and you're destroying the family name. If I could find out you're embezzling, so could anyone else. What if it gets out?"

Edmund scoffed. "It won't get out, and anyone else who

knows about it or even threatens to go public with it, I'll take care of them."

"I don't want you taking care of shit," Drake said. "I want you out of here. I'm not trying to take anything away from you. You want to keep the money you stole? Fine. I won't tell Dad. Just do the right thing and resign. Or else, I'll be forced to go to the board and remove you."

"You'd never go to the board and risk this leaking."

"If it means saving the company and keeping this family out of prison, you bet your ass I would. I won't stand by and allow you to steal from the company or the family anymore."

Edmund leaned back in his chair, a smug look on his face. "Then I guess you're going to do what you have to do."

Drake's heart sank. He had hoped that Edmund would see reason, but it was obvious that he wasn't going to make it easy for him. He took a step forward, planted his hands on the desk and leaned forward, his eyes locked on Edmund's.

"Damn you."

* * *

It was the faint noise that woke Cecily. Her heart raced as she moved her hand from underneath the pillow and slowly opened the drawer of her nightstand. The soft sheets rustled against her skin as she moved, and an unfamiliar sense of fear washed over her. But she pushed it away as she felt the steel grip of the pistol in her hand. In one motion, she turned and shot up in bed, her gun aimed into the darkness. The room was silent, save for the faint noise that had woken her in the first place. She strained to hear it again.

Someone was in here. Someone was watching her.

She threw back the duvet and climbed out of bed. As soon as her feet made contact with the cold wooden floor, she peered around the room, her eyes struggling to adjust to the darkness. Another noise, this one barely audible, came from the walk-in closet. She inched toward it, her heartbeat speeding up with each step, but the steady grip of her gun led the way and kept her calm. She paused outside the ajar doors of the closet, slowly reached her free hand out and wrenched the doors open. In the next instant, a dark figure pushed her down and ran out.

Her grip on the gun was lost as she hit the floor, but Cecily quickly regained her composure and scrambled to find it in the dark. She found it, stood to her feet and chased after the intruder.

The landing outside her room was pitch black, and she couldn't see where they had gone. She pointed her gun in front of her, walking down the hall and hugging the wall. Suddenly, she heard a creak behind her and spun around. In the darkness, a figure loomed, and Cecily's instincts took over. Her finger was on the trigger, but before she could react, a hand pushed her arm up in the air. She fired the gun into the air, and the sound echoed like a cannon throughout the hallway.

"Jesus Christ!" Drake hissed as he tightened his hand around her wrist and pulled the gun from her grasp. "What the hell are you doing?"

"Drake?" She asked, both surprised and relieved to see him. "What are you doing here?"

"I was working downstairs in the study and was just coming up to bed. Answer me. What the hell are you doing?"

"Someone was in my room," she said.

"And you thought you'd take care of him by shooting blindly in the dark?"

"What's going on? Is everything all right?"

That was Gianna's voice, followed by more footsteps coming onto the landing. Before Cecily could react, Drake tucked her gun in his back waistband and turned on the lights of the upstairs hall.

"I heard a gunshot," Leo said as he came out of his room in his pajama pants.

"Everything's fine," Drake said. "Cecily heard something, but it was only me."

"I know what I heard," Leo insisted.

Drake shrugged, looking around. "Well as you can see, no one's been shot. I checked with Dad's nurse before I came upstairs, and he's sound asleep. Maybe we should all do the same."

Leo shook his head and waved a hand before returning to his bedroom, obviously too tired to argue any more about it. "Goodnight, all."

Gianna stayed behind and looked between Drake and Cecily.

"Goodnight, Gianna," Drake prodded.

"Goodnight," Gianna said and turned and rounded the corridor to return to her room.

The moment she heard Gianna's door close, Cecily tried to step past Drake and back inside her room, but he gently took her by the arm and pulled her back to stand in front of him.

"What's this all about?" He asked in a hushed whisper.

"I told you. Someone was in my room. They were hidden in the closet, pushed me down and ran off. I was trying to chase them down, but you stopped me and now whoever it was is probably long gone."

"Who do you think it was?"

"I don't know, but whoever it was, knows where I sleep."

"He shook his head. The security here is state of the art. There's no way they could've got inside."

"Well, apparently they did, and instead of questioning me,

you should be alerting your security and have them search the grounds."

He studied her for a moment longer and then pulled his cell phone from his pocket. He scrolled to a number and dialed. When the other end picked up, he started to bark orders.

"Cole, we have the possibility of an intruder. Search the grounds but be quiet about it." He paused and spoke to Cecily. "Did you get a good look at him?"

She shook her head. "It was too dark."

"I don't have a good description," Drake relayed to his head of security. "Yeah…let me know if you find anything."

He disconnected the call then silently gestured for Cecily to return to her room. She turned and hesitated at the threshold of the open door and stared into the darkened room. She knew whoever had been there was gone now, but what was stopping them from coming back?

Drake reached around her, flicked on a lamp, and the sudden rush of light startled her.

"Everything all right?" He asked.

"I'd feel better with my gun."

He snorted. "So you can almost shoot me again? I don't think so."

Cecily looked around the room and turned her attention on the open door to the large walk-in closet. How long had the intruder been standing there in the dark watching her?

Drake cleared his throat. "If you want, you could stay—"

Cecily whirled around to look at him. "I could stay where?"

His intense gaze matched hers, and they both stood there pondering what he had been about to say.

"There are other guest rooms," he said, his eyes hardening and his tone now brusque.

"No," she said. "I'll be all right."

"Suit yourself, but your door has a lock on it. Use it."

"I will. By the way, I'm going to Vegas with you."

He frowned. "The hell you are. I'm only going to check on the progress of Olympus. You need to stay here and keep working on finding that account."

She stepped into his space. "If you really think I'm going to let you out of my sight for a week, you're insane. Wherever you go, I go."

She realized too late that she was standing too close to him, dressed in only a strappy chemise and matching bottom that fit her like underwear. He'd noticed it too and was looking at her with a fire in his eyes she willed herself to ignore.

She stepped back into her room. "I'll start packing in the morning. Good night."

Without waiting for a reply, she firmly closed the door in his face and leaned against it. She listened to his footfalls on the landing as he headed in the direction of his own bedroom. Then came the faint sound of a door opening and shutting, and she finally let out the breath she'd been holding.

CHAPTER SEVENTEEN

Cecily stepped out of the private jet onto the tarmac at the international airport in Las Vegas. The dry heat of the desert kissed her face, and an early summer breeze ran through her curls. She was regretting the dark pantsuit she chose to wear with the sun in full force. What she wouldn't give for a light and airy sundress.

"I hope you have more options besides those pantsuits," Drake said, as if reading her mind. He came to stand behind her as he de-boarded the jet. "You're not going to be very comfortable in this weather."

He was wearing a tan linen suit and white dress shirt opened at the collar. It was casual attire for him, but there was no mistaking his wealth and privilege.

"I'll be fine," she said stiffly, mentally promising herself to find a women's clothing store.

He smiled and gestured ahead of them to a waiting limousine parked just a few feet away.

"Let me show you Olympus."

As the limo weaved through traffic, Cecily stared out the

window, taking it all in. The city was a cacophony of activity, towering hotels, and endless crowds of people.

"That's it," Drake said, leaning over and pointing out the window.

Cecily turned in the direction he pointed and had to restrain herself from widening her eyes and staring in awe at what would undoubtedly be a gorgeous hotel, spa and resort. The cranes and scaffolding covering the Olympus construction site signaled that something big was on the rise.

The driver pulled into a private parking lot. The two of them got out, and Drake handed her a white construction helmet for protection. Cecily's heels clicked across the marble floor of the unfinished Olympus lobby, the sound echoing through the massive 60-story atrium. She gazed upwards, shielding her eyes from the Nevada sun streaming through the glass walls. Drake guided her through the expansive ground floor, describing the amenities to come.

"The lobby bar will be decorated with mosaic tilework. The guest rooms will have marble baths with 24-carat gold plated fixtures and floor-to-ceiling windows overlooking the Vegas skyline."

They stepped outside to a terraced patio overlooking a tropical oasis below.

"I'm calling this the Garden of the Gods pool area with lagoons and waterfalls, poolside cabanas, and the centerpiece —a massive statue of Poseidon emerging from the pool with his trident," he said with unmistakable excitement.

"This is quite a project," Cecily said, as she envisioned the sprawling paradise when it was finished and imagined herself lounging by one of the infinity pools.

They entered the casino, which even unfinished, had soaring marble columns and more mosaic tilework across the floors.

"For high rollers, there will be a private VIP lounge with

complimentary champagne service and butler attendance," Drake described.

At last, they reached the spa, and Cecily's eyes lit up at the indoor mineral pools, steam rooms, and what would be a fully-equipped salon. This was an amenity that appealed to her—a peaceful oasis from the constant stresses of work and life. She could already imagine indulging in a massage, sauna and beauty treatments.

"We'll have a rooftop yoga terrace as well," Drake added, watching her.

"It—it's going to be beautiful." She paused and met his eyes. "You should be proud."

"You sound surprised," he said.

She shook her head. "With your money, I'd be surprised if it was anything short of spectacular."

He frowned at that, but Cecily turned away and continued to admire the surroundings. It was apparent that he was determined to make this resort the crown jewel of the Strip, catering to the most affluent visitors with over-the-top opulence and amenities. But in reality, she was very impressed with what Drake did with his money and the beautiful things he managed to create. However, she wasn't about to tell him that.

In the back of her mind, she thought that maybe it would've been better if she'd just stayed in San Francisco looking for that account. What was she achieving by jetting off to Las Vegas with Drake just to see his new hotel?

They left the construction site, and in less than forty-five minutes, they arrived at their hotel. As they moved through the lobby, a man in a dark tailored suit approached them. Cecily could see Drake recognized him immediately as he flashed a charming smile and extended his hand.

Drake turned to Cecily. "This is Cyrus Wilkes. He's Chair of the board of the company. Cyrus, this is Cecily—my wife."

Cyrus clutched her hand and planted a kiss on the side of her cheek. "I heard Drake was married, but he kept it a private affair. It's nice to meet you, Mrs. Morgan."

"It's nice to meet you too," she said.

"It's good to see you Drake," Cyrus said. "I was told you would be in Vegas, and I hope you don't mind, but I've taken the liberty of making a dinner reservation for you and your lovely wife to join Selina and me."

Cecily instantly felt Drake stiffen beside her, and she knew he was going to politely decline the offer. But she wasn't about to miss out on a possible connection to Edmund.

"We'd love to join you," she said.

Cyrus beamed with satisfaction. "Great. The reservation is for seven-thirty in the Oak Lounge."

* * *

Drake paced the floor of the suite, feeling apprehensive. He wasn't in the mood for this dinner because he already knew what it would be about—fulfilling Edmund's promises. He came here to oversee the construction of Olympus. He just wanted to move past any and everything that reminded him of Edmund and his practices. But the past seemed to have him in a vice grip. And with Cecily going after Edmund's offshore accounts like a dog with a bone, it seemed he would never escape his brother's shadow.

The doors to the second master bedroom opened, and Cecily walked out. She did her best to appear no-nonsense and business-like, but it was difficult to pull off with what she was wearing.

He'd ordered the designer dress from one of the hotel's high-end boutiques downstairs. It was a beautiful shade of emerald green, with a fitted bodice that accentuated her curves and a full skirt that flowed gracefully to the floor. The fabric was made of a soft, silky material that looked luxurious against her skin. The dress had delicate spaghetti straps that crossed over her back, leaving her shoulders bare. The neckline was a classic V-neck, plunging just enough to be alluring. Her breasts were full and pushed together to create cleavage that was making him forget all about Edmund and the past. That seemed to happen a lot around her. She had a knack for giving him a temporary escape and he was looking to prolong it.

"You look beautiful," he said, meaning every word of it.

She pointedly ignored his compliment. "I only agreed to this dinner because he worked so closely with Edmund."

He chuckled. "Is that money the only thing you think about?"

Her brown eyes blazed. "It's the only reason I'm here."

She then looked down at herself, picked up the skirts of her gown and dropped them in a huff. "This dress is a little too much for dinner, isn't it?"

He chuckled again, amused by her obvious discomfort. "If you think the dress is too much, you're going to think these are completely over the top."

He then handed her a velvet box he'd been clutching in his hands.

"What's this?"

"Just something to go with the dress."

She slowly opened the lid of the box. He watched her and could detect the moment she set her eyes on the glittering emeralds and diamonds.

She shut the lid tight, shook her head and went to hand the box back to him. "I can't wear these."

He took the box from her but only to take out the necklace. "Turn around."

"Drake," she protested.

"Turn around."

She hesitated then slowly turned and faced her reflection in the mirror. He removed the white opal necklace she always wore, put it to the side and then delicately placed the emerald necklace around her neck. It was the centerpiece of the collection with a large emerald cut stone set in a delicate white gold chain. Surrounding the emerald were smaller diamonds and emeralds, arranged in an intricate pattern that resembled a blooming flower.

"I can't wear this," she said again, shaking her head.

"Yes, you can," he countered. "You wanted to come on this trip with me, so I'm going to need you to look like the wife of a billionaire."

He stared at her reflection, his eyes tracing the curves of her body.

"This was your idea," he said, speaking into her ear. "Play your role."

Cecily's face flushed with anger, but she didn't say anything. Instead, she took a deep breath, picked up the earrings and bracelet and put them on.

"Shall we?" He asked, extending his hand.

She ignored his outstretched hand by marching past him and exiting the suite. Despite the anger in her strides, he noticed the skirts of her dress moved gracefully, its silky fabric whispering against her skin.

CHAPTER EIGHTEEN

Dinner at the Oak Lounge started off with introductions and polite conversation, but it took a different turn the moment Cyrus told Drake about a business relationship he was hoping to restart.

"Gavin Reyes. He and Edmund did a lot of business together," Cyrus said. "Edmund was days away from signing a deal with the Reyes family before he was killed."

"The Chilean businessman. I remember him," Drake said, his voice calm and measured, despite his irritation.

"Did Tara send you the details about the deal he and Edmund had worked out?"

"Yes, she did."

Cyrus frowned. "I never heard back from you about it."

"That was my answer," Drake said.

Cyrus looked to Selina and laughed heartily. "Drake, come on. You can't be serious."

"I am serious. I killed the deal and had Tara send our apologies to Gavin and his team. Edmund was charmed by the Reyes family money. I'm not. It's blood money."

"That's insane," Cyrus protested.

"Why do you say it's blood money?" Cecily asked.

Drake looked to her. "The Reyes family has a history of using children in the copper and diamond mines they own. Gavin only wants to partner with me to make his company look good. It's a PR move."

"Okay, so he's trying to turn his tainted image around," Cyrus said. "Isn't that what you're doing with your family's company?"

"That's exactly what I'm doing, but I'm not changing the image and still doing the illegal shit in the background."

The knowing look on Cyrus's face gave Drake pause. What did the son of a bitch know that he didn't?

The answer came almost instantly. Leo.

"Try and see reason," Cyrus said. "This is a good deal."

"What's in it for you?" Drake asked. "What did Edmund promise you?"

Cyrus looked to his wife again and then over to Cecily with slight discomfort. "I was promised a small bonus for introducing Gavin to Edmund."

Drake snorted. "Small as in tens of millions."

Cyrus's eye twitched. "I've been very loyal to your family and this company, Drake, and I expect fair compensation for that."

"I'm sure you do."

"I'm taking this deal to the board," Cyrus said. "They'll agree to this. Otherwise, we may have to talk about extending the IPO."

Drake stilled. "Are you threatening me?"

"No, of course not. We want the same thing: we both want what is best for the company, and Edmund's deal is great for the company."

"Even if it means getting into bed with sharks," Drake finished. "The answer is no. I'm not taking money from people with that history."

"Christ, Drake that was his father, and he's trying to turn things around just like you."

"That's not what I heard. I have contacts in that company. He's not turning around anything, and I won't do business with him."

Cyrus spoke, his voice tight with frustration. "I don't understand why you're being so stubborn. Leo promised him that we would resume business dealings and fulfill Edmund's promises. It wouldn't look good for you to back out now."

Drake's eyes narrowed. "Leo isn't in charge. I am, and I say kill the deal."

"Then good luck with the IPO."

Drake didn't even realize he started to rise from the table. He was going to take Cyrus by the scruff of his neck and yank his short ass out of the chair. No one fucked with his business.

"Drake."

The haze of red filling his eyes, dissipated instantly when he felt a soft touch on his arm. He looked down and saw Cecily's hand was clutching him. He looked from her fingers to her eyes and saw she was silently communicating with him to let it go. He slowly sat back down.

Cyrus cleared his throat. "Listen, Drake. I know a lot was left on your shoulders when Edmund died. I can respect what you're up against." He rose and took his wife Selina's hand. "Let's pick this up back in San Francisco."

Drake didn't respond but only pierced him with a look that told him to get lost.

"Enjoy the rest of your evening, both of you." He took Cecily's hand and kissed it. "It was a pleasure."

"Thank you," Cecily said and smiled at him and Selina before they left.

Once they were gone, Drake snatched his arm out of her grip and quietly seethed.

CHAPTER NINETEEN

Leo tipped the doorman generously as he glided through the open glass doors of Club Nova. As he stepped inside, the thumping bass reverberated through his body. The dance floor was adorned with colorful lights, casting a haze over the dancing crowd, and the air was thick with the scent of alcohol and perfume.

Leo's eyes scanned the room, searching for his target. He spotted her in an elevated VIP section, her silhouette outlined against the soft glow of the surrounding lights. He made his way through the crowd, navigating the sea of bodies that moved and swayed to the music.

As he approached the VIP section, he couldn't help but admire her beauty. Her fire red hair cascaded down her shoulders, framing a face that held both elegance and a hint of mischief. She was dressed in a form-fitting white tank dress that accentuated her curves, exuding a confident allure that drew glances from both men and women alike.

Leo took a deep breath, steeling himself for what lay ahead. He had rehearsed this encounter in his mind countless times, imagining the various ways it could play out. He knew he had to be careful, to tread the line between persuasion and manipulation. This was a delicate game, one that he had to win.

He approached Elise, his footsteps muffled by the pulsating music. She looked up, her eyes meeting his, and he saw a flicker of surprise cross her face.

"Leo," she said, her voice tinged with a mix of curiosity and wariness. "What brings you here?"

Leo flashed her a charming smile. "I own the place. Mind if I join you?"

She gestured to the seat beside her, and Leo removed his suit jacket and sat beside her. The music seemed to fade into the background as he focused all his attention on her.

"You shouldn't be here all alone."

"I came here to be alone," Elise said.

"I doubt that's true. It looks like you could use some company."

"You're not the Morgan I'm looking for," she countered.

"Sorry, he's in Vegas with his new bride overseeing the Olympus project," he said, signaling for the server to bring him his usual. He then turned back to Elise and snapped his fingers as if just remembering something.

"Didn't you used to accompany Drake to Vegas?"

She looked at him with disdain but ignored the bait.

"It's not right, you know," he continued, turning on the charm. "You put years in with that man, and he never once mentioned marriage."

Elise smiled thinly, and her eyes grew cold, but he could see her shell cracking with each nerve he struck.

"What do you want, Leo?"

"Only what's rightfully yours and what's rightfully mine."

"The company," she concluded.

He nodded.

"And how exactly am I going to help you get the company? I'm not an employee, and Drake doesn't discuss business around me anymore."

"The key word is *anymore*," Leo said. "He used to. He used to take you on trips with him, dinners with him to meet clients, didn't he?"

She eyed him, her curiosity returning.

"Just tell me what was talked about."

"And what do I get in return?" She asked, leaning forward.

He smiled. "The Morgan you're looking for."

"He's married."

"It doesn't have to be forever. I have ways of facilitating a separation."

She sat back in silence.

"So, what do you say?"

She put her wine down. "The fact that you have to come to a woman to do your bidding tells me what I always knew."

His gaze hardened. "And what's that?"

"That your father knows what he's doing. He chose the right CEO. You know, you don't need to be like Edmund."

"I'll take that as a no, but thanks for the free therapy."

"I care for Drake," Elise said. "And maybe one day he'll see that. But I'll get him back on my own. I don't need a woman to disappear to make it happen."

Leo accepted defeat for now and stood, shaking his head in pity for her. He pulled his money clip from his pocket and peeled a few hundred dollars from it.

"It's a shame such a beautiful woman like yourself has so much loyalty to a man who obviously has loyalty for someone else."

He dropped the money in the middle of the table. "I know how it feels to play second, and I'm tired of it. Let me know when you get tired of it, too."

Walking away from the VIP section, Leo cast a final glance over his shoulder. Elise was still staring at him, a mixture of curiosity and uncertainty in her eyes. He had her. Now, he just needed to wait.

CHAPTER TWENTY

rake and Cecily returned to the hotel suite without a word. After Cyrus and Selina left, he'd remained quiet through the rest of their dinner. However, she'd known him long enough to know he was ready to erupt at the slightest opportunity.

He used the keycard to open the double doors of the suite and waited for her to go in ahead of him. Cecily strode in and placed her matching green clutch down on a side table by the door. She then turned and saw that Drake had closed the double doors, but he'd remained standing by them, deep in thought.

"Do you want to talk?" She asked.

He shook himself free of his thoughts and strode past her to the large living area. "No. I can handle Cyrus."

"Could he really stop your company from going public?"

Drake removed his dinner jacket and threw it over the sofa. "He could delay it, but he's not only a board member, he's also a shareholder, and he stands to make a lot of money when this IPO goes through. I'm not worried about him."

He was worried about Leo, Cecily guessed. That part was

left unsaid, but she could sense that his youngest brother making moves behind his back is what had Drake's face pinched in anger.

Drake removed his cufflinks, tossed them onto a nearby table and rolled up the sleeves of his white dress shirt. He went to the bar, poured himself a drink and then stood by the floor-to-ceiling windows and looked down at Las Vegas boulevard alive with lights, cars, and pedestrians.

After another drawn out silence, he spoke again. "I don't know if there will ever be a day when I'm not paying for Edmund's mistakes or cleaning up after him."

"Don't start doubting yourself," Cecily said, coming to stand behind him. "Every decision you've made has been for the good of the company."

He tossed the drink back in one gulp and then turned around to look her. "Including marrying you?"

"That's right," she said, lifting her chin. "You may not like my methods, but when this is all over, you'll see it was the right decision."

He looked around the room. "You like this suite?"

She frowned at the abrupt change in conversation. "It's very nice."

"The Olympus is going to be an all-suite hotel. Every room will be one, two and three-bedroom suites."

"What about the penthouse?"

I'm saving that for a two-story Presidential suite. It'll be about 10,000 square feet with a private pool, spa, and movie theater."

"Sounds expensive."

He laughed and then stepped closer to her. "It is, but you can have it all for free since you're my wife."

"By the time that hotel is completed, our marriage will be over."

He shrugged. "Maybe."

She shook her head. "There is no *maybe*. As soon as I get that money, I'm out of here."

Drake reached out and stroked his finger from the side of her cheek, down to her neck and even further down to the décolletage of her dress. He then quickly snaked an arm around her waist and pulled her into him.

"Why did you come here with me, Cecily?"

"You know why, and it's a good thing I did, or else I wouldn't have known about Edmund's back room deals and Leo's moves. Your family loves keeping secrets, but what you don't understand is that I'm damn good at finding them."

"And what about the secrets you're keeping?" He asked. "Don't fool yourself into believing you can hide anything from me."

"My secrets have nothing to do with you."

He used two fingers to lift the emerald necklace from her neck. "Maybe I should get you to talk to Cyrus. He couldn't seem to keep his eyes off you during dinner. Then again, I don't blame him."

She narrowed her eyes. "So, what is this? Another proposition? You want me to seduce a married man so that your billion-dollar deal goes through?"

His eyes raked over her body. "More or less. Don't you think it's about time I get something out of this arrangement of ours?"

She pushed out of his grasp and tried to slap him, but he gripped her wrist and tightened his hold until the glass he'd been holding slipped from his hand and crashed to the tile floor between their feet. Drake paid no mind to the shattered glass but tightened his hold on her.

"You really think I'd let you near Cyrus?" He asked. "I wanted to put my fist in his jaw each time he looked your way a few seconds too long. I told you, I'll handle him, and as for you seducing a married man—that's exactly what I want you to do." He released her, moved his hands around to grip her ass and brought her directly to his hard-on. "Seduce *this* married man."

Cecily willed her features to remain expressionless. She refused to be sucked into his seduction even though the feel of him through his trousers was turning her on to the point of making her senseless.

"How much do you think Edmund squirreled away in that account?" He asked. "Two hundred million? Three hundred million?"

"Maybe."

"I can give you that and more," he said, his voice now deep and husky.

She didn't flinch at the insult. "I'm not for sale, Drake, but it must be nice to know that money and power can buy you anything you want—even people."

He tilted his head to look up and down the length of her body before returning to her face with his hardened gaze. "Apparently, it can't buy me you."

"If I were you, I'd keep my mind off my body and on the business because I promise you Drake, if I don't get what I want, your family and your company will go down!"

She punctuated the threat by putting a hand to the back of his head and pulling him in for a kiss. She didn't know what possessed her to do it. Maybe it was being trapped in his arms, the sexiness of his voice, his indecent proposal to buy her, or even the way the bulge in his trousers seemed to swell with each word. But the moment their lips met, she knew she'd screwed up. She succumbed to the memory of Houston when he was kissing her just like this. It was hot and heavy to the point where she couldn't think. She'd been lost the moment he touched her, and she was on her way to the same fate now.

Drake wasted no time. He responded by deepening the

kiss and claiming her mouth. He bent at the knees, lifted the skirts of her gown and picked her up with ease. He backed up, sat her on the bar, spread her legs and moved between them without breaking the kiss. They clawed at each other, both seeking dominance and praying the other submitted.

But even as Cecily's body cried out for more, her mind wouldn't let her go there. Over and over the same thoughts rang loud in her head: He is a means to an end. He serves a purpose, and that purpose is to help Tony.

Drake reached for the back of her gown, slowly unzipped it, and she knew that once her breasts were exposed to him, his intense gaze, and his mouth, she would be lost.

It took every ounce of her willpower to tear her lips from his and push him back. Without looking at him, she hopped off the bar top, marched into her bedroom and slammed the door.

CHAPTER TWENTY-ONE

"Welcome back, Mr. Morgan," Tara greeted, handing Drake his usual cup of coffee. "How was your trip?"

"Productive," he said, gratefully taking the coffee. "What's my schedule like today?"

"You have a nine-thirty meeting with R and D, a photographer from the Chronicle is coming to take your picture for the profile at eleven…"

Drake sat at his desk, trying to focus on her words when he noticed Cecily exit the elevator. He gave her a private office at the opposite end of the hall to do her work, and as she walked by, she gave a slight nod as a good morning. Drake returned the subtle greeting, wishing he could say and do more. But with so many eyes on them, getting up to follow after her, unbuttoning that blazer to get at her breasts and fucking her against the wall in that small office would draw too much attention. The vision had been on his mind the entire ride to work, which only made him grateful they didn't drive together. All he wanted was to finish what they started in Vegas.

They were in a beautiful suite all to themselves, and he had wanted nothing more than to see her come undone as she had that night in Houston. But Cecily was so strait-laced and focused only on their business and her goal that she wouldn't allow herself to drop the inhibitions and just be with him.

But the big question was: Why did he even want her to drop her inhibitions? What they had was a strict arrangement, so why couldn't he just let her do what they agreed and get her out of his life? He shouldn't find anything about her remotely attractive, especially when she only represented his betrayal of Edmund.

"Mr. Morgan?"

He put his attention back on Tara and saw that she was watching him curiously.

"I'm sorry. What did you say?"

"I just asked if everything was all right. You seem distracted."

Drake sensed movement behind Tara. His gaze swung past her, and he caught the eye of his head of security, Cole. By the look of intensity in his eyes and the way he was striding with purpose to his office, Drake assumed the intel he'd been waiting for had arrived. He stood and beckoned him in with a wave of his hand.

"I'm fine," he said to Tara. "Let's pick this up later. I need to speak with Cole."

She nodded and exited through the door Cole held open for her.

"Good morning, sir," Cole said, coming forward. "I have some information for you about Mrs. Morgan."

"Don't call her that," Drake snapped.

Cole looked taken aback and then recovered quickly. "Sorry, sir. I mean, Ms. Reed."

They moved to the large sitting area of the office. Drake

sat in the loveseat while Cole chose an armchair and promptly placed his laptop on the coffee table. After tapping a few keys, he turned the screen toward Drake, who read a few sentences and then looked up at Cole in question.

"This is it? This is all you've been able to find on the man she was meeting? His name?"

"I'm sorry, Mr. Morgan, but whoever this man is, he moves like a ghost. All I've been able to find out is his name is Antonio Green, his date of birth and birthplace, and the fact that he served in the military—Army Rangers to be exact."

Just like Cecily, this man's background information was scarce.

"He stays here in the city, somewhere in Potrero Hill," Cole continued. "I'll get you an address as soon as I can."

Drake's mind raced along a track as it formed a picture, and he didn't like what he was seeing. Not one fucking bit. He'd married Cecily to allow her access to his family and his company's financials, but where did Antonio Green fit in? Were they partners? Was he looking for the same thing as Cecily?

"This stays between us," Drake said, resting his hands between his knees as he tried to formulate a plan of action.

"Yes, sir, but there's something else you should know," Cole said. "I had a hunch and called a friend who works for the FAA. They sent me the manifests for all flights from San Francisco to Houston around the time of your trip, and Antonio Green's name and picture show up with the same flight number as Ms. Reed. Here's his picture."

"They were on the flight together?" Drake asked.

"It looks that way."

"Why?" He asked, not really expecting an answer.

"I want to up your security," Cole said.

"No. I don't want her to guess that something's up."

"Sir, you can't trust her."

"I know, but she's not after me."

Drake knew what her intentions were, and it wasn't to harm him.

"She wants Edmund," he continued. "But since she can't get to him, she wants the next best thing."

"Who?"

"Whoever he was working with," Drake said, absentmindedly going through the digital photos and paused when he saw one of Cecily entering the brick building in the Tenderloin.

"Did you find out what this place was?"

Cole nodded. "Yeah, but it's not what you think."

CHAPTER TWENTY-TWO

*O*ne year ago...

"Explain to me why I had to drive an hour in traffic to meet you at your beach house?" Cecily asked, irritation flowing through her.

"I offered you the company chopper, but you refused," Drake said with a shrug.

"Because it wasn't necessary. No matter the inconvenience I'm perfectly capable of driving myself."

He arched one brow in curiosity. "Does my wealth bother you so much?"

She rolled her eyes. "Of course not. You can make as many billions as you want, and it wouldn't matter to me. Just tell me why I'm here."

"You said you wanted to meet up to talk about Edmund."

"Yes, but we could've met at the usual spot to do that."

He gestured around them. "It's private here. This place has been in the family for years, but I'm the only one who comes out here. I'll be staying here for the night, and the chef is making the best oysters and mussel dish I've ever tasted. Would you like to join me?"

She frowned. "What are you playing at?"

"Nothing."

"Is this why you asked me to come here? To ask me to dinner?"

He shrugged. "We can talk while we eat. You do eat, don't you?"

She turned her attention now on the tide coming in. The wind whipped strands of hair from her bun into her face, and she whisked them away.

"I need to go," she said, suddenly.

"Why?"

"Because this is inappropriate."

"There's nothing inappropriate about this. We can't talk business over dinner. I do it all the time when I'm making deals. You want to hear my update? Have dinner with me."

She let go a hollow laugh. "Okay, let's get something straight. I'm not some model, actress, or social media darling you met at a party. We're not dating. The only thing we have in common is your brother, Edmund. That's what I'm here for. So, tell me what I need to know, so I can get home before traffic becomes unbearable."

He thought about challenging her but told himself it was only his ego reminding him that he didn't take no for an answer. Instead, he decided that he'd accept defeat—but just this once.

"I confronted Edmund last night about the embezzlement. I demanded his resignation."

She looked at him aghast. "Why the hell would you do that?"

"Because he's my brother, and I owe him at least that."

"It wasn't your place. I need that offshore account, and if he knows about me, he'll disappear."

"He doesn't know about you," Drake countered. "He

refused to resign, and he's still in the city. I wanted to give him a chance to make it right, but he's too fucking arrogant and greedy."

Cecily turned her attention to the ocean once again, seemingly lost in thought. As the sun dipped lower toward the horizon and cast a warm glow over the water, Drake studied the fiery determination in her eyes. He hated to admit it, but he admired her.

"Time is running out," she said. "There's got to be a way to get me into your company's financials. I can find the account before Edmund withdraws from it."

"Not without drawing attention," Drake said. "The one thing I'll say about my brother is he knows about everything going on in the company."

"Let me think of some options," she said. "Anything else?"

He shook his head.

"Then I'll be in touch," she said. "Don't do anything until you hear from me."

She started to leave, but Drake reached out and quickly took her hand to stop her. She looked down at his hand clutching hers, and he realized it was the first time he touched her.

"For the record, I know you're not a model, actress, or social media darling. You're not someone looking to be seen with the latest eligible bachelor. That's why I asked you to have dinner with me. I knew that sitting across the table from you would've felt like a real date and not a photo opportunity."

Something flickered in her eyes, and he allowed himself to hope for just an inkling that she was going to accept his invitation. She was right. It was inappropriate of him to ask her, but he couldn't help how much he was drawn to her. In fact, he resented it, but he couldn't deny it nonetheless.

Then the flicker vanished, and she resumed her usual mask of aloofness as she slipped her hand from his grasp.

"We're not dating, but I'll take a raincheck on a business dinner. Enjoy your oysters, Drake."

CHAPTER TWENTY-THREE

Hank pulled to a stop in front of the same brick building Drake had seen Cecily enter a month before, got out, rounded the car and opened the door. As Drake stepped out onto the curb, he saw that the streets were lined with trash and broken glass, and the sound of shouting and car horns echoed in the air.

"Are you sure you'll be all right here, Mr. Morgan?" Hank asked.

"I'll be fine. Just wait here for me."

He looked up at the building which had certainly seen better days. Its faded paint and cracked windows were a stark contrast to the skyscrapers in the distance. The once vibrant brick facade was now weathered and stained with years of neglect. The windows were covered in a thick layer of grime and dirt, obscuring any glimpse of what was inside. A rickety fire escape clung to the side of the building, rusted and precarious.

He pulled open the metal door and instantly the smell of old books and dampness hit him. To his right, was a young man behind a desk scrolling through his phone. He noticed

Drake and obviously saw by his attire that he didn't belong in this neighborhood.

"Can I help you?" The young man asked.

"I was actually looking for someone. Cecily Reed."

"Oh sure, Cee!" His eyes lit up in recognition. "She's in the back. Just follow the hall all the way down until you get to the last door on the left. She'll be in there."

"Thank you," Drake said, now more confused than ever.

To his left was a gymnasium where several boys of different races and ages played on a basketball court. The floor was scuffed from years of play, and the hoop was ragged and leaning dangerously to the side.

He started down the hall and as he passed by doors, he could see through the glass partition they were rooms with children. There was a computer room that had computers as old as he was and another room reserved for dance or ballet. There were other rooms for various activities, and he came to the realization that this was a recreation center for kids. When he came to the last door to the left, he looked inside and saw the children sitting at easels with art supplies.

He soundlessly opened the door and for a moment, all he could focus on was Cecily at the center, sitting at her own easel and concentrating on her work. He'd never seen her look so alive and full of joy as her paintbrush moved over the canvas with ease. But when her eyes slowly slid from the easel to him, the joy instantly vanished.

* * *

Cecily tossed her paintbrush down, grabbed a rag to wipe her hands and stood.

"Keep at it, guys," she said, not taking her eyes off Drake. "I'll be just outside."

She stalked past him and out into the hall. Once he

cleared the threshold, she closed the door behind them and unleashed the anger she'd been keeping at bay.

"What the hell are you doing here?" She asked. "How did you even know where I was?"

"I followed you here a few weeks ago," he said, and his forthright tone and the fact that he didn't even try to bullshit her shocked her.

"Why are you following me?"

"I told you, I have a right to know who I'm married to."

Her eyes narrowed to slits. "If this were a real marriage, I'd agree with you, but it's not. Whatever I do on my personal time is none of your business."

"Why are you so angry?"

"Because this is..." she waved her hands to signal the building and everything in it. "This place, my time with those kids, is all mine. It has nothing to do with you, with Edmund, the account, nothing! You want to have your high-profile security team keep tabs on me, that's fine. But keep your distance."

He amused himself with her indignance for just a moment then looked down at his watch and pulled his cell from his pocket to make a call.

"Hank, change of plans. Take a break and pick me up in about an hour."

Cecily felt her blood begin to boil as he reached for the doorknob. She put her hands over his to stop him from twisting it open and stepped into his personal space.

"Go back to your boardrooms and billion-dollar deals, Drake. This is not your life."

"But it is yours," he said. "And I want to see it."

He twisted the knob and moved past her to enter the room. The kids instantly looked up from their easels and regarded him curiously. He gave them all a nod and a smile and removed his overcoat to lay it across a chair. He then chose an empty easel to sit at and picked up a paintbrush.

"So, what are we painting?" He asked no one in particular.

"What we want to be when we grow up," Tina, a young girl with vibrant, wavy black hair said.

Drake looked over to see what she was painting. It was a rudimentary figure of a girl with black hair like hers sitting at what looked to be a piano.

"I can see what you want to be," Drake said and looked over in the corner where a piano sat. "Do you practice on that?"

She blushed. "I don't know how to play, and we don't have anyone here at the center to teach me."

Without another word, he put down his paintbrush and motioned her to follow him to the piano that was collecting dust.

"What are you doing?" Cecily asked, coming forward.

"I play a little," he said, sitting down at the bench. "Will the music disturb the class?"

Cecily looked around and saw that the other kids looked eager and excited for him to play. Shooting him an angry look, she finally relented and motioned for Tina to go ahead and join him. The young girl practically jumped up and ran over to the piano. He scooted over to give her room and as Cecily made her way back to her easel, the sound of music filled the room, stopping her in her tracks and forcing her to turn and look at him with amazement.

The piano was in dire need of tuning, but it was hardly noticeable as Drake's fingers moved effortlessly across the keys, coaxing out a melody that filled the air. The notes flowed from the piano, each one blending seamlessly with the next. The melody filled every corner of the room with its beauty, and Cecily found herself drawn to it and the man creating it. As the music came to an end, she was left feeling both uplifted and melancholic. The beauty of the sound lingered in the air, the notes still ringing in her ears long after the last chord had faded away.

The sound of applause broke Cecily from her trance, and she couldn't help but clap as well. Drake looked to the children and nodded humbly. His eyes then found Cecily, and his stare was penetrating.

"You said you play a little?" She quipped.

He smiled and winked at her before returning his attention to Tina.

"Now, let's start with the basics," he said and began demonstrating one key at a time.

Cecily moved back to her easel, and as hard as she tried, she couldn't stop gazing over at Drake as he led the young girl through the basic keys. It was a side of him she'd never seen before, and it was so different from the way he normally portrayed himself. It was certainly a different image from the one she created of him. It showed her a more human side of him when all she wanted was for him to remain just a suit. Now, she couldn't stop looking at him, but what made her want to run and hide was that he kept looking her way, too.

CHAPTER TWENTY-FOUR

Drake sat in his office, feeling drained. He had just finished a conference call with the department heads, and he longed to take a much-needed break out of the office. But when he saw Leo coming his way, he remembered he'd promised him a lunch meeting.

"Are you ready?" Leo asked. "I made this reservation for 12:30."

"Are you going to tell me who we're meeting?"

"You'll see when we get there. Just promise me to keep an open mind and listen."

That gave Drake pause, but rather than stand there and force Leo to tell him what this was all about, he mentally decided that the sooner he got this over with, the sooner he could take a drive to the coast and give himself that break he wanted.

Out of nowhere, he thought about inviting Cecily along. He knew she was holed up in her temporary office, searching for Edmund's embezzled money. Maybe she'd like a break, too. But he knew instantly, she'd just refuse him. Ever since he showed up at the center and saw her in a way she hid from most people, she'd been avoiding him.

He sighed, stood and grabbed his jacket and informed Tara that he would be out of the office for the next two hours. By the time they rode the elevator down to the lobby and climbed into the waiting car outside, Leo's nonstop chatter about the client they were going to meet, and how good it would be for the business, had become white noise.

Drake was barely listening, his mind still preoccupied with thoughts of Cecily. They were supposed to be partners in name only, but lately, Drake had been feeling something deeper for her—feelings he'd thought had been eradicated with the end of his last marriage. If he was being truthful, he'd begun to feel something more for Cecily long before they were married. Their arrangement had begun with deceit, but somewhere along the way, he'd become interested in exploring the woman behind the hostile exterior.

As they drove through the streets of the Financial district, Drake tried to push aside his thoughts and focus on the business meeting ahead. But when they arrived at the upscale restaurant and he saw the client they were meeting with, he realized why Leo had been so secretive about it all.

Gavin Reyes and Cyrus Wilkes sat at the table watching him expectantly.

"What the fuck is this?" Drake asked, barely moving his lips.

"It's just lunch," Leo murmured. "All I ask is that you hear what he has to say."

As Drake and Leo approached the table, Gavin and Cyrus both stood and shook hands with the brothers.

After Edmund's death, Drake had taken over and wasted no time in severing ties with a lot of the shady business relationships that Edmund had been involved in. Gavin was one of those clients. Apparently, Drake hadn't made himself clear enough in Vegas when he told Cyrus this same thing. Now, it appears Cyrus had gone to Leo for reinforcement. This wasn't just lunch with a potential client. This was an ambush.

After Drake shook hands with both Cyrus and Gavin, he sat down and didn't say a word.

"I appreciate you meeting with me, Drake," Gavin said. "Let me start by saying I understand your reservations about working with my company with the tainted history we have. But let me assure you that just like you, I've taken over for my father, and I'm committed to turning everything around."

Drake looked to Leo, Cyrus and then to Gavin. He then made a silent gesture for Gavin to have a seat, and a collective sigh was heard around the table. However, after twenty minutes of Gavin speaking and Leo and Cyrus cosigning everything he said, Drake voiced everything that was on his mind.

"I get that you had a close relationship with my brother, and you're expecting me to continue that. But like you said, I'm trying to do new things in my family's company, and even though you say you are, too, my investigators tell me different."

"Drake—" Cyrus tried to interrupt.

But Drake forged on. "Yes, I had your company investigated, and from what I can see, you have no intentions of removing those children from your diamond and copper mines, and if I had the slightest bit of influence in Chile, I'd fucking destroy you for that."

Rage came across Gavin's features, but Drake didn't care one bit. He had to pause and physically restrain himself from reacting violently to the man. The thought of orphans working in his mines made him think of Cecily and her childhood in foster care—vulnerable and helpless.

"It seems my brother and Mr. Wilkes made certain promises to you, but they are promises I don't intend to keep. Let's make sure this is the last time I say it." He stood from the table and buttoned his suit jacket. "Enjoy the rest of your lunch, gentlemen."

As he left them all slack-jawed, he heard Leo excuse himself and assure them he'd be right back. As Drake stood outside the restaurant, waiting for his driver, Leo marched up behind him, his face twisted in anger.

"What the hell was that, Drake?" He asked. "You just turned down a lucrative offer and for what? Your fucking morals?"

Drake was scrolling through his phone for messages and then slowly turned to his brother. "Don't ever set me up like that again. You know how I feel about Gavin Reyes. I ended that relationship for a reason, and I don't need you or Cyrus questioning my decisions."

"Since when did you get so high and mighty? His money is just as good as anyone else's," Leo said. "Edmund had no problem with him."

"Edmund isn't here anymore. I'm the one who's running this company, and there are other ventures we can partner with. So, either get on board or get out of the way."

They stood there staring at each other, both refusing to back down.

Leo huffed. "Fine. Go back to the office, but I'm going back in there and finishing this deal. If you want to fire me, call my fucking lawyer."

Drake watched his brother go and for the first time, realized how much he hated Edmund for the destruction he left behind.

CHAPTER TWENTY-FIVE

As soon as Cecily stepped out of the limousine and onto the sidewalk, she paused to admire the colorful murals adorning the buildings in the quaint and up and coming San Francisco neighborhood.

Almost immediately, reporters surrounded her, taking her picture and shouting questions at her. She lowered her head to keep away from the camera flashes and nearly stepped back inside the limo. Then she felt Drake clutch her hand.

"Give them a few smiles and then we can go inside," he whispered into her ear and pulled her closer to him as they posed for the cameras.

Cecily was not used to being in the limelight, and she never expected to be thrown into it even as Drake's wife. She wondered if he got the irony of what was happening here— they were posing as a happily married couple for the cameras but also posing for his family and his employees.

When they entered the Fuego, Cecily had to admit she was impressed. The place was housed in an historic building with large windows and the trademark Victorian architecture. As they stepped inside, she was greeted by a bustling atmosphere with the sound of chatter and clinking glasses filling her ears. The interior was decorated with a blend of modern and rustic touches, with brick walls and hanging light fixtures. The aroma of spices wafted through the air, making her mouth water.

"The couple of the hour have finally arrived," Gianna said, gliding up to them and looking stunning as the hostess. She leaned into Drake and gave him a kiss on each cheek and then stepped back to eye Cecily.

"You look amazing," she said. "I haven't seen you dressed up since your wedding."

"Thank you," Cecily said.

She tried to ignore Drake's eyes tracking up and down her knee-length, beige bandage-wrapped dress with its off the shoulder neckline that showed off her cleavage. He'd been doing it all evening, and she wanted to tell him to stop it because the hunger in his eyes was only making her feel warm inside.

When she'd come out of the shower that evening, she'd found the Valentino dress laid out across her bed. It was the same move he'd made in Vegas. While she'd been planning to put on one of the simple black cocktail dresses she'd bought years ago at a clearance sale, Drake was still on a mission to make her play the part of his wife—the wife of a man of considerable wealth. Yes, the designer dress was gorgeous, and he obviously knew her size very well, but this part of the plan to pose as his wife made her uncomfortable. This was all fake, but Drake was making her wish it wasn't.

"Your table is over here," Gianna said and led them to their reserved table in a private corner of the restaurant. A server was already there waiting to pull Cecily's chair out for her and hand Drake a wine menu.

"Do me a favor and make sure you sample everything,"

Gianna said. "The house wine, an appetizer, entrée and dessert."

Drake chuckled. "We'll try, but don't be surprised if I ask for a to-go box."

She winked. "I have plenty of them ready. Enjoy."

Drake started to pick up his menu and then lowered it. Cecily felt him stiffen beside her and when she followed his gaze, she noticed Leo striding over to them.

"Drake," Leo said, stiffly.

"Leo."

Leo turned to Cecily. "Good evening."

"Hi, Leo," she said, wondering what was crackling between the brothers.

Leo turned back to Drake. "I thought you should know Gavin is excited about the deal. He wants to work with our family again, and he wanted you to know that his family's history is not the way he does business anymore."

"You can believe his promises all you want, but know that I have the final say. I can kill this deal before it even reaches the board," Drake gritted.

Leo nodded. "Then I guess it's a good thing I have Cyrus in my corner. He has sway with the board."

The way Drake eyed his brother was lethal. "The two of you think I can be persuaded in this deal, so let me make it plain for you: It's not going to happen. Now, leave before I fuck up Gianna's opening."

Leo's eyes burned as if ready for confrontation, but in the end, he bowed slightly to Cecily and left. The server quickly approached the table, and Drake ordered a bottle of the house wine.

"Gavin Reyes, again," Cecily said once they were alone again. "You know I can look into—"

"No," he snapped. "I don't need your interference in this,

too. I'll handle Leo, the board and Gavin Reyes on my own. Got it?"

"Got it," she said stiffly and then put all of her attention on the menu before taking another look around to admire the décor.

"She did a good job with this place," she said, trying to ease the tension.

Drake took his eyes off his menu and looked around as well. "Yeah, she did."

Cecily smiled wryly. "Then again, she did have a nice budget, thanks to you."

She went back to reviewing the menu but could feel that his eyes were now on her. She slowly looked up and faced him.

"What?"

"Why do you do that?" He asked.

"Do what?"

"Constantly bring up my wealth."

She shrugged. "Do I?"

"Yes, you do, and it always sounds like an insult coming from you. I can't help I was born into money no more than you can help being born…"

He trailed off and her gaze narrowed. "What were you going to say? I can't help I was born poor?"

"No."

"Because I wasn't born poor. Both of my parents were teachers. No, we weren't rich, but we didn't starve."

"I wasn't going to say that."

"Then what were you going to say?"

"That you can't help being born with a chip on your shoulder."

She laughed. "I don't have a chip on my shoulder."

The server came with a bottle of red wine and two glasses.

He allowed Drake a look at the label and when Drake silently approved, he poured each of them a glass. Another server appeared with bread and olive oil to place in between them. After Drake ordered their appetizer, the two servers left.

He took a sip of his wine and then set the glass down. "You have something on your shoulder. If you weren't born into poverty, then what is it about me that bothers you so much?"

"It bothers me that men like you and your brothers have no appreciation for the life you have. Look at Edmund. He had more money than he knew what to do with, and even that wasn't enough. He needed to steal more."

"I'm not Edmund."

"And Leo, running a billion-dollar business as a COO, but he wants the top job only to run it with ruthlessness."

"I'm also not Leo."

"No, but I guarantee there's something. There always is." She picked up her napkin from her lap and threw it down on the table. "I'm going to use the ladies' room."

"To be continued," Drake said, as he stood from his chair in respect.

Cecily didn't really need to use the bathroom, she just needed to get away from him. Recently, being in Drake's presence was making her feel as if she were suffocating, especially when he was sitting so damn close. They were nearly touching elbows in that dark, romantic corner at a table for two.

She went into the restroom, which was also decorated in high-end Italian style, complete with a restroom attendant. She stared at herself in the mirror and silently asked herself what the hell she was doing here. This wasn't her world. Her world was numbers, late nights, and takeout Chinese food from the restaurant below her apartment. She didn't belong here in Fuego, in this Valentino dress and especially not in a mansion in Presidio Heights.

But this could be your world if you wanted it to be.

There was the inner voice again, reminding her of a truth she refused to acknowledge. But she shut it away, washed her hands, and accepted the towel from the attendant. She then left the restroom, mentally preparing herself to return to Drake. But just before she rounded the corner to enter the dining room, a hand clamped down on her wrist and brought her back into the shadows. She turned around and came face to face with Tony.

"You look great," he said, admiring her appearance.

"What are you doing here?" She asked in surprise.

"You promised me periodic updates," he said.

"There's been nothing to update."

"I still need to hear from you, Cee. I told you to not underestimate this family."

She rolled her eyes. "I can handle Drake."

"You're sure about that?" He asked, gesturing over her shoulder.

She turned and saw Elise, looking gorgeous in a simple but stylish little black dress that was almost certainly a designer label. It hugged her curves as she approached the table where Drake was sitting. She leaned over him, whispered something in his ear and slipped a piece of paper into his suit jacket. Cecily tamped down her rising jealousy, wondering where the hell it had come from.

She turned back to Tony and shrugged. "This marriage is for two things: getting access to Edmund's offshore account and the name of his partner. I don't care about Drake's private life."

Tony dropped the mocking grin, put his hands to her waist and pulled her close to him. "I'm just looking out for you. This plan of yours could blow up in your face at any time. You're risking yourself for—"

"For you," she finished. "Once I find that account, they won't have any choice but to listen to you. You'll get your reputation back. Stop worrying and just let me do what I do best."

Tony nearly said something in response, but she watched as his eyes trailed from hers to something slightly above her head and stayed fixed there. When he dropped his hands from her waist and stepped back, Cecily turned around and inwardly cursed when she saw Drake standing just behind her.

"The appetizer is here, and it's getting cold," Drake said, his hard green eyes on her.

"Sorry, I just ran into a friend of mine. I'll be right there."

She should've known he wouldn't be dismissed that easily. His piercing eyes slowly moved from her to Tony.

"I don't think we've met," Drake said.

Tony stepped forward with his hand outstretched. "Antonio Green, but I go by Tony. It's a nice place you've got here."

"Thank you, but it's all Gianna's doing. I just supplied the money." Drake shook his hand and then looked to Cecily. "How long have you two known each other?"

Tony spoke up again. "Cee and I are old friends. She was kind enough to give me an invite."

"Really? She never mentioned you," Drake said. "She's always struck me as a loner."

Tony shrugged. "I guess you don't know your wife as well as you think you do."

"Tony, don't," Cecily scolded.

"No, he's right. I need to take the time to get to know you better. Starting now. It was good to meet you, Mr. Green," Drake said and possessively took Cecily's hand. "Come eat your dinner. Then we need to get going because I have an early meeting."

"Good night, Cee," Tony said.

She cast an angry glare over her shoulder at Tony as she allowed Drake to lead her away.

CHAPTER TWENTY-SIX

*D*inner between them was silent, yet so loud with all the words they wanted to say to each other. But neither of them spoke the rest of the evening except to tell Gianna how delicious the food was when she stopped by their table. Drake finished his meal, asked the server to make the dessert to-go and told Cecily that he was ready to leave.

The moment she stood from the table, he took her by the hand and practically pulled her behind him, sparing only a few words of congratulations to Gianna on a successful opening. Finally, they were outside, and he breathed in the cool air wafting in from the bay. For a moment, the deep inhalation of breath was enough to wash away the tension and fury that seemed to be closing in around him.

Then it instantly returned when Cecily snatched her hand from his.

"What's going on with you?" She snapped.

"Smile for the cameras and then get in the limo," he gritted.

She challenged his stare for a beat, spared a few smiles

and waves for the reporters and then climbed into the back seat. Drake slammed the door and then walked to the other side where Hank held the door open for him. It wasn't until they were a mile from the restaurant and traveling through the city streets when she turned on him.

"I don't know what that was about back there, but it can't happen again. How many times do I have to tell you that my personal business is mine?"

"Then keep your personal business out of my line of sight," he said. "I don't need to see your personal business copping a feel in my restaurant."

Quick as a flash, she leaned over, dug her hand into his suit jacket and plucked out the handwritten note Elise had placed inside. He should have snatched it back, but her being so close to him and putting her hands on him had shocked him into immobility. He sat there powerless as he watched her read the brief note which was an informal invitation to Elise's apartment.

"You have plans this evening?" She asked, balling the piece of paper up and throwing it at him.

Drake caught it with one hand, tossed it to the ground and slid over to her side of the limo. Cecily tried to back up, but Drake snaked his arm around her waist and snatched her close. Her breasts pressed up against him and her cleavage heaved with indignation.

"You want to question me about a fucking piece of paper? Tell me about him!"

"I already did. He's a friend and colleague."

"He's more than that. You've been working with him. You've been meeting him."

She boldly met his gaze. "He's none of your business."

He tightened his grip around her waist, bringing her even closer to him. "I have ways of getting the answers I want. I can have my security team pay him a visit in that shitty flat in Potrero Hill."

Her eyes slightly widened at the realization that he knew where the man laid his head, but he omitted the part that he was still waiting on Cole to give him a physical address.

"Leave him out of this," she said.

He wanted to feel triumphant, but the sight of her fear ignited a blazing jealousy inside of him that was deep and primal. Whoever this man was, he meant something to her.

His gaze traveled from the fire in her eyes down to her cleavage nearly popping out of that dress as her breasts were crushed against him. It hadn't been the first time that night he'd admired her or thought of different ways of removing the dress. He'd fantasized about how she'd look in it the day he had Tara order it. But the moment she'd come down the stairs wearing it, he realized his fantasies hadn't done her justice. Every curve she loved to hide behind those dark pantsuits was on full display. She often wore loafers, but now she was wearing heels that made her legs look incredible. Without warning, he gripped both of her legs now and brought them up to his lap.

"Hank, close the privacy window," he said, not taking his eyes off her.

"What are you doing?" She asked, sounding breathless as the dark window slowly rose, and they were essentially alone together.

"Whatever I want," he said and slid from the seat to the floor of the limo to kneel directly in front of her.

Her eyes widened with shock as his hands slid her skirt up past her thighs and over her ass.

"Drake, no. We're not doing this."

His hands trailed up further, found the lace of her panties and pulled them down over her thighs and knees. Jealousy, fury and lust were fueling him. She wanted to defend this Tony to him? He'd show her he didn't come second to any man.

"Drake…"

"Keep your eyes on me," he commanded, lifting one of her legs and placing it over his shoulder. Then his face went in, inhaling her sweet scent.

He looked up and saw her eyes were darting between him and the privacy window. He knew she feared that any moment, it would roll down and Hank would see her legs spread wide, her mouth agape, her eyes rolling to the back of her head and her face twisted in pleasure at what he was doing to her. But as he licked and sucked, he felt her growing wetter, and it was obvious that the thought of someone seeing his face buried between her thighs excited her.

Drake let out an animalistic groan from the fact that her excitement was now all over his mouth. She put her hand to the back of his head and pulled him in deeper. He wanted it, and goddammit, she was going to give it all to him.

She bit down on her lower lip to keep the scream from erupting, but she couldn't stop her body from convulsing. He continued to lap at her greedily, wanting to taste every bit of what he'd done to her until finally, her convulsions slowed.

When he started to turn his head and kiss her soft brown thighs, he knew he'd gone too far. He thought he'd had her in his control when in truth, she had him in her clutches. He raised himself back onto the limo seat, poured himself a drink from the minibar and downed it in one gulp. Then he remained very still, watching the scenery outside without daring to touch her. Beside him, he could hear the rustle of fabric as she slid back into her panties and pulled her dress back down over her hips and thighs.

He hadn't expected that. He'd done it to her as a punishment, but she enjoyed it and what's worse, he'd enjoyed it too —very much.

The moment Hank rounded the driveway of the mansion and pulled to a stop at the front door, Drake escaped from the car leaving Cecily behind. He stalked inside and was immediately greeted by his father's nurse.

"Good evening, Mr. and Mrs. Morgan."

Drake put on a restrained smile. "Good evening, Hannah. How's my father?"

She laughed. "He kept me up longer than he should've trying to beat me in 'Go Fish'. But he's finally asleep. How was the opening of the restaurant? Your father was so sorry he couldn't make it, but his headache seems to have passed. He hopes to make it up to Gianna."

Drake nodded, feeling Cecily's presence close behind him. "It was a success. Good night."

"Good night to you both," she said, heading to her private rooms in the opposite wing of the house.

Drake watched her go and then hesitantly turned to Cecily who was now watching him with a multitude of questions in her eyes.

"Good night," he said simply, ignoring the look and whatever was on her mind.

He climbed the stairs to his room and shut the door. He then leaned his back against it and pounded his head against it over and over.

"You fucking idiot," he cursed himself.

God, he could still smell and taste her scent on his mouth, and he couldn't resist licking his lips.

He should've tossed that piece of paper the moment Elise slipped it into his jacket pocket. Married or not, he wasn't interested in seeing her. For over a year, Cecily had been the only woman that had consumed his thoughts to the point where he was ready to explode. That brief but hot episode in the limo had brought him back from the edge, but it hadn't quenched his thirst in the least. But taking her to his bed had not been part of his plan when they married. This was a business arrangement and nothing more than that. When it was all over, they would go their separate ways.

But being in the same house with her right now wasn't doing anything for his nerves. He needed to take a drive somewhere, get lost somewhere in the city and come back when he could look at her and think straight.

He pulled open the double doors to his suite and just as his luck was going, she opened the doors to her bedroom across the hall at the same time. She hadn't changed out of that dress yet, but she'd removed her heels, and her small feet hugged the carpet as she stood there looking indignant.

"Are you leaving?" She asked.

"I'm going for a drive." He stepped into the hall and against his better judgment, he made his way to her. "You want me to stay?"

"I don't care what you do."

She wanted to be defiant. That was okay because he could play along. For now.

"You and I both know that's not true." He was upon her now and with her heels gone, he dwarfed her short and thick frame. "From the way your thighs were cradling my head in the limo, something tells me, you'd like to continue where we started."

He said it to embarrass her, but her eyes remained a still, dark brown but something in them flashed. She wasn't embarrassed, just like she wasn't embarrassed in the limo. She was turned on. She liked it when he spoke to her that way. The strait-laced money girl had a kink for dirty talk. She was full of surprises, and Drake was going to have some fun with her.

He reached one hand out and slowly stroked her cheek

down to her neck and to the curve of her breasts where it stayed. His eyes moved up and glued to hers. There was wanting in them. He used his other hand to reach behind her, pushed down the handle of her bedroom door and opened it. He backed her into the room, slowly shut the door behind him and leaned up against it.

"You do want me to stay," he said, but remained still against the door. He wouldn't touch her. He'd let her make the move.

The next thing he felt was her body pressed up against him and her lips seeking his. He wrapped his arms around her waist and claimed her mouth.

"Say it," he urged between kisses. "Tell me to stay."

She brought her arms around his neck, and he moved his hands to the back zipper of her dress to undo it. She stepped away long enough to slip the dress over her curves and let it pool at her feet. She then reached behind her with one hand and unsnapped the hook to her bra. Drake watched mesmer-ized as the piece of lace hit the floor and looked up to see she was now wearing nothing but that white opal necklace.

Drake went for her breasts, cupping them in his hands and taking turns licking and sucking each nipple gently.

"Tell me to stay."

Cecily put her hand to the back of his head, ran her hands through his hair and arched her body into him, urging him on with her soft moans. He promptly gripped her by the ass with both hands, lifted her in the air and tossed her onto the bed.

"Say it," he demanded once more.

She inched away from him toward the headboard, but he slowly trailed after her, while at the same time removing his tie, his dress shirt, and trousers. The moment he stood naked before her, he leaned down, grasped her legs and pulled her to him. He reached down and yanked her panties over her thighs, down her legs and tossed them to the side. He then covered her body and entered her with a swiftness coupled with an ease that had them both calling out for more.

"Stay," she finally cried out, but it wasn't necessary. He wasn't going anywhere.

CHAPTER TWENTY-SEVEN

*D*ays turned into weeks, and Leo threw himself into his quest to gather incriminating evidence against Drake. He scoured financial records, dug into the company's operations, and even hired a private investigator to follow Drake's every move. But no matter how hard he searched, he couldn't find the smoking gun he needed to bring his brother down.

With each passing day, Leo's determination grew, fueled by a mix of ambition and resentment. He yearned for the power and control that being the CEO would bring him to the point that it consumed him.

One evening, he was leaving the office, deciding this was a perfect time to visit Nova and drown his discouragement in alcohol and women. Then his phone his chimed.

"Hello?"

"Leo." The voice on the other end was unmistakably Elise's. "We need to talk. Meet me at Salvador's in an hour."

Leo's heart quickened its pace, a rush of adrenaline surging through his veins.

"I'll be there," he replied, his voice barely containing his excitement.

As he hung up the phone, Leo couldn't help but wonder what had changed Elise's mind. Had she finally realized the truth about Drake and where she stood with him? Had her loyalty finally begun to crumble?

An hour later, Leo entered Salvador's, a popular speakeasy nestled in the heart of the city. The air was heavy with the scent of whiskey and the low hum of conversation. The atmosphere was dimly lit, with exposed brick walls, vintage décor, and a timeless charm.

Leo's eyes scanned the bar, searching for Elise, and he spotted her sitting in a secluded corner with an untouched martini in front of her. Her eyes met his, and she beckoned him to join her.

As he approached, he couldn't help but notice the hardness etched on her face. The sparkle that once inhabited her eyes had dimmed, replaced by a hint of resignation. He took a seat opposite her and leaned forward with a mixture of curiosity and concern.

"Everything all right?" He asked.

She sighed. "I wasn't going to call you at all. I actually invited him to my apartment after the restaurant opening, and like a fool, I waited hours for him to show."

Leo waited her out, knowing she needed this moment to come to grips with what she was about to do.

"You were right. Drake hasn't been loyal to me, and I can't see myself continuing to be loyal to him."

He resisted the urge to pump his fist in triumph. Finally. He knew this woman held secrets about his brother that no one else had. After all, she had been intimate with him years after his divorce from Jasmine, and no one knows secrets more than an intimate partner. It was why Leo chose to frequent high-end escort services. He paid the money, got what he needed, and there was never an expectation of anything more—there would never be a woman walking around holding his secrets.

Elise's eyes met his. "It's not what you think. I don't have any evidence of any wrongdoing. Drake is serious about leaving all of Edmund's ugly deeds in the past. But I do know something that might shake things up."

"What is it?"

She took a deep breath then expelled it. "About a year ago, Drake and I were on a date. Right before we were about to order, he got a text and stepped outside the restaurant. I was annoyed because it was the first time in a while I had him all to myself, and I didn't want any interruptions."

"But he left, and I watched him. Our table had a view of the street outside, and I thought he was just going to stand there and take the call. But he kept walking further down the street. I tried to see where he'd gone, but it was dark outside, and I lost him."

Leo frowned. "Don't tell me he left you and never came back. That doesn't sound like Drake."

She shook her head. "No, but he was gone for a while, and I was getting impatient. So, I told the waitstaff I'd be right back, grabbed my purse and left in the same direction he'd gone. I saw him, but he was further up the street. I nearly called out to him, but something stopped me."

Elise paused and Leo saw that her eyes seemed to look through him as though she were watching the memory play out like a movie.

"I saw him—with her."

"Who?"

She focused her eyes on him again. "His wife."

Leo leaned forward in his seat to be sure he'd heard her right. "Wait a minute. You're saying you saw Drake with Cecily?"

She nodded.

"What were they doing?"

"Talking, but it looked like something more. Drake looked so angry with her, but the way he was grabbing her had me feeling so fucking jealous."

"Why?"

She finally took a sip of her martini and leveled her gaze at him. "Because even though he looked ready to throttle her, I recognized his body language. He wanted her."

Leo's mind raced as he contemplated the possibilities this revelation held. This was a year ago, but Drake told him he'd met Cecily only a few months before when he was in Houston. He made it sound like it was love at first sight. But if Elise was to be believed—and something in Leo convinced him she was telling the truth—it would appear his brother and Cecily have known each other for a long time. If that's the case, why would Drake lie about that?

A surge of anger and confusion washed over Leo. He needed to find out who Cecily was. He pulled his cell from his pocket and scrolled to a number. When the call was answered, he spoke in a rushed tone.

"Cole, I need you to look into Cecily Reed for me."

"I already have, Mr. Morgan. It's the first thing your brother had me do," Cole said.

Leo paused. Drake had done a background investigation on her?

"All right. Bring me everything you have on her."

"Anything I should know, sir?"

"I just want to know more about her. And by the way, Cole, this stays between you and me. Drake doesn't need to know about it."

There was the slightest hesitation on the other end before Cole replied, "No problem."

Leo ended the call and tucked his phone away.

"You're still determined to be head of the company, aren't you?" Elise asked.

He peeled two large bills from his wallet, put them in the middle of the table and stood, preparing to leave.

"I told you. I'm only going after what's rightfully mine."

Elise offered him a small, sad smile. "Just remember, Leo, power can be addictive. Don't lose yourself in chasing it."

CHAPTER TWENTY-EIGHT

When Cecily woke the next morning, Drake wasn't beside her. She figured he must have snuck out some time in the early hours after their second round of what she didn't want to admit was unbelievable sex. She stretched under the soft linen and then rolled over and reached for her cell phone on the nightstand. When she saw the time, she instantly got out of bed to take a quick shower.

As she lathered herself, she thought of Drake's hands all over her body last night and how hot he'd made her feel. When her hands trailed from her breasts and even further down, she thought of his lips and tongue not denying a single inch of her. Then she covered her face with her hands and groaned under the steaming hot water. God, she'd really messed things up.

It was nearly ten in the morning when she descended the stairs, and from the lack of chatter coming from the dining room, she figured the rest of the family was sleeping in as well on this Saturday morning. She grabbed her purse and car keys and hurried out to the driveway and jumped inside her car. Once she peeled away and was heading to the other side of the city, she breathed a sigh of relief that she hadn't seen Drake. She couldn't deny that being with him had been amazing, but she also couldn't deny that last night was a catastrophic mistake.

When she got to Tony's apartment, she trudged up the old, rickety stairwell while trying to build up her courage to go inside and face him. From the very beginning, he'd voiced how stupid and foolish it was of her to marry Drake, and last night in the limo and in her bed had proved him right.

Just as she raised her hand to knock, the door swung open, and Tony stood there with a garbage bag in his hands and a surprised expression on his face.

"Hey Cee, I didn't know you were coming by."

"I should've called first, but I really need to talk to you," she said.

The warmth in his eyes cooled to concern. "Sure, let me just take this trash to the dumpster, and I'll be back in a minute."

He opened the door for her to go inside, and she waited while he made the short trek to the dumpsters outside. She looked around the small apartment that was serving as a temporary hideout for him until their job was complete. The apartment was small and dingy with peeling paint on the walls and a musty, yet faint cigarette odor hung in the air. There were cardboard boxes scattered around, and the only natural light came in from the medium-sized barred window at the far corner of the room.

She wondered if he would ever feel safe enough to return to his own more modern and cleaner apartment on the other side of town once she found the name of Edmund's partner and where the money was stashed. Edmund had driven him underground, and it had been Cecily's number one goal to get Tony's life and reputation back for him. Now, given her actions last night, she wasn't so sure if she'd jeopardized that.

She gave the living area another once over and noticed something on the countertop that separated the kitchen from the living area. She walked over to it and saw it was a matchbook with a recognizable logo. She'd seen the same logo last night.

"Everything okay?" Tony asked as he reentered the apartment.

Cecily picked up the matchbook with the name *Fuego* written in script and turned to face Tony.

He looked at it and chuckled. "I grabbed a bunch of those last night before I left. Nice place. I can see it's a little too rich for my blood, but the food was pretty good."

"Why were you there, Tony?" She asked. "And please don't tell me it's because you were worried about me."

His amused smile slowly disappeared, and his features became stern as he let go a sigh.

"Fine. If you really want to know, it's because I'm not sure you have it in you to finish the job—at least not anymore."

She frowned. "Are you kidding? I've been busting my ass for months trying to find that account."

"I'm not questioning your skills, Cee, but I am questioning your judgment. Marrying Drake is one thing, but the trips to Las Vegas, the date night to his fancy restaurant—"

"That was all business."

"Was it?" He asked, challenging her. "Because it sure didn't look like business when you saw him with that red-headed bombshell."

She stood there silently seething while he continued to read her like a book.

"I know and remember that look very well," he said. "That wasn't business. That was jealousy, and jealousy means you care. So, my question is, why do you care about him? He's nothing but a job—a means to an end."

"I haven't lost sight of what we're trying to do here," she said.

"I hope not because once we find that money, we'll find out just how far the Morgans' reach is, and we can bring this family and the entire company down."

She frowned again. "This is about Edmund. There's no need to bring Drake and his company down, too. He agreed to this marriage to help me dig in deep, and I promised him that after this was all done, I'd walk away, and he could go through with the IPO."

He shook his head with disappointment. "You sure made a lot of promises to that man without talking to me."

"I gave him my word, Tony."

"I need you to come back from fantasyland. You really think Drake Morgan is squeaky clean, don't you? That man used to supervise beatings and worse. They were ordered by Edmund, but Drake wasn't innocent. Any rival competitor that seemed to step on their territory, they'd crush them."

She stepped forward. "You know all that about him, but yet you still made it your business to go to that opening last night? You're supposed to be laying low, but instead you're putting yourself in Drake's crosshairs. He's not even supposed to know about you."

"I told you why I was there."

"And I don't need you looking in on me. Fall back and let me do this my way."

He went silent for a moment and then without warning, he surged forward and gripped her forearm.

"What the hell are you doing?" She asked, trying to break free, but Tony only tightened his grip.

"I think you forgot who you were talking to," he hissed in her face. "I don't fall back. I don't take orders. You do what I say and stick to the goddamned script. No more trips, no more fancy dinners. You find that money and give me what I've got coming to me."

He then wrenched her arm free, causing her to stumble back. Cecily's eyes widened with pure shock. Never had he put his hands on her, never had she seen him so furious and never had he turned that fury on her. She felt her stomach lurch at the fear that she didn't know him as well as she thought she did.

Tony ran both hands down his face and then rubbed the top of his head before exhaling a breath. "Cee, I'm sorry. I didn't mean that. This has been going on too long, and the stress has gotten to me."

"I need to get back."

She headed to the front door, but Tony was right on her heels as she opened it. He blocked her path and peered down at her with eyes silently begging her forgiveness.

"I'm sorry," he said again. "I don't know where that came from, but I shouldn't have grabbed you like that. It was uncalled for. But I'll say this again. Marrying Drake Morgan was a dangerous idea, and that family isn't the type to let blackmail go. You need to finish the job and get the hell away from them."

Without saying another word to him, she adjusted her sunglasses, left the apartment and jogged down the stairwell, the knot in her stomach growing with each step.

CHAPTER TWENTY-NINE

*D*rake strode through the halls of the mansion, disappointed to not find Cecily there. He'd hoped they would have breakfast together. Knowing her, she wanted to forget all about last night, but he wasn't going to let her do that. He wanted to talk about it. A deeper part of him wanted to know where they went from there. This had been the second time he felt himself inside her, and it only made him long for her again and again.

He started to search for her in the lounge, but stopped on his way there when he came to the doors that led to the conservatory. He stood at the threshold to admire his mother's sleek, black grand piano. That morning he caught Cecily in here, he'd stayed back and for just a few moments, watched her run her fingers along it. He enjoyed seeing how she looked standing there under the sunlight, arrested by the piano's beauty. For years, he'd ignored the piano, but ever since that day at the rec center with Cecily's students, it had renewed an urge in him to play it and remember his mother.

Seeing that no one was around, he stepped into the conservatory, sat down at the bench and hesitated his fingers over the keys. Then all at once, he let his fingers dance, and a melody filled the air. The music moved him and spoke to him in a way that words never could. It was both haunting and uplifting, enveloping him in warmth and comfort. Every note spoke to him, telling him a story that only music can convey. He allowed himself to become lost within it, his mind free to wander as he let the melody wash over him. But he wasn't too far gone to not sense her standing behind him. Although he wanted to face her, he continued to play.

"It's beautiful," Cecily said.

"It was my mother's favorite tune," he said.

"Why don't you play more often?"

He shrugged. "This was her piano. Playing it reminds me of her, and sometimes the memories aren't so great."

The conversation lapsed as Drake played on and the tune reached a crescendo and then back down.

"You were gone when I woke this morning," she said.

"I went to get us some coffee and bagels from this place I like."

She chuckled. "You have an entire staff to make you coffee and bagels."

"Sometimes I like to let them sleep in, too. You've been gone long. Your coffee is cold, and your bagel isn't fresh anymore."

"It's okay. Thank you for the thought."

"Are you just coming from the rec center?"

"Why do you ask that?"

"Because I noticed that's where you go when you have a lot on your mind."

"And you think last night put a lot on my mind?"

"Well, I can understand the position it puts you in."

His fingers paused over the keys and the abrupt silence that filled the room was deafening.

He turned on the bench to look directly at her. "Is that where you went?"

"No."

"Did you go see him?"

She hesitated before answering. "Yes."

His eyes stayed fixed on her, but he didn't say anything.

She sighed heavily. "He's involved too, Drake. I have to keep him informed of everything."

"Is that right? So, you told him we fucked?"

Her eyes blazed, but she didn't have the right to be offended. He was the one who returned to an empty bed after an indescribable night of passion, and she'd gone to see another man. He didn't mean to use that word to describe what they did and how she'd made him feel. If he was honest with himself, it had been more to him than that. He just didn't know if it had been more for her, too. He wanted to rile her because she was once again erecting a wall between them.

"Did you?"

"Of course not," she gritted.

"Why? You don't want him to know you screwed up?"

She sighed again. "Is this what you want to do? Do you want to argue about Tony?"

"No. I wanted to have bagels and coffee in bed with you and continue what we started last night, only this time in my bed."

"You know this can't happen again."

"You said that in Houston, but here we are."

"I mean it, Drake. This complicates things."

"You really don't want to let yourself enjoy being married to me, do you? It's only temporary. Take advantage of the perks while you can."

She stepped close to the piano bench, her back now stiff as she towered over him in anger. Her eyes were brimming with fire, and he wanted nothing more than to pull her down onto the bench beside him and take her into his arms. Why the hell did she affect him so much?

"Houston was different," she said. "We were both alone, under a lot of pressure after your brother died and needed a way to relieve it."

"Were we?"

"What?"

"Were we alone?" He asked.

"Yes. As soon as I heard you'd flown out of San Francisco International, I found out where you'd gone and booked the next flight."

"And your boyfriend just happened to be on the same flight."

"Tony isn't my boyfriend, and he didn't come with me to Houston."

Drake could feel his temper surging. "He was on that plane. What was the plan? You seduce me into marrying you and he was there in case I refused?"

"I have no idea what you're talking about."

He stood from the bench in a flash causing her to back up. "I have the damn manifest. Tony Green was on that flight with you."

"I wasn't aware of that."

Her denial was sending him over the edge because she was too damn difficult to read, and he couldn't tell if it was the truth or if it was all just an act.

He gripped the back of her neck and pulled her face in close to his. "Last night, I discovered one kink of yours. You like dirty talk."

"Let go of me," she said.

"Did I just find another one? What was he doing when you and I went upstairs to my suite?"

"Drake—" she warned.

He moved in until his lips were barely touching her ear. "Was he watching us? Is that what you like?"

"Go to hell!"

She shoved him away, but that only sent him back a few feet. In the next second, he was once again upon her, but this time he did what he'd been wanting to do since she walked in the conservatory. He pulled her into his arms and overpowered her with a kiss that made him feel like he was on fire. He could feel her struggling to break free, but he kept his arms tight around her waist. He didn't want to let her go. Once again, anger, jealousy, and passion overwhelmed him, and he needed her to extinguish it all.

He tore his lips from hers but kept his face close. "I want you all to myself, do you hear me? When I hold you, when I kiss you and definitely when I fuck you, it's just you and me!"

Her struggle against him lessened, and her body began to relax. He took advantage by lowering his head and putting his lips to the curve of her neck, and deeply inhaled her scent. The perfume she wore last night had faded, but it was still there. A memory rushed in, flooding his mind with the image of her legs and thighs cradling his waist, his hands touching her soft brown skin amid his moans and her cries of pleasure.

"Drake," she whispered, and it was his undoing.

"Ahem."

A throat clearing was like the sound of a dinner gong. Cecily sprang away from him, and he was left feeling abandoned. Drake turned to whoever had interrupted them and saw it was Gianna. If it had been a member of the house staff, they would've withered from the fury in his eyes, but Gianna's gaze and stance were firm and defiant.

"Sorry to interrupt. The staff heard shouting and didn't want to come in." She divided a look between them and then turned to Drake. "Cole is here. He said you two have a meeting."

"Thank you," he said. "Tell him to wait in the study for me. I'll be right there."

Gianna looked at them both again, repressed a sly smile and closed the door behind her. Drake turned to Cecily who was discreetly adjusting her clothes after he roughed them up from groping her.

"Give me about thirty minutes," he said. "This won't take long."

"And then what?" She asked. "We head upstairs to your huge master suite?"

He didn't answer that, but there were only two words replaying in his mind that was raucous and deafening: Hell, yes.

"Cole is waiting for you," she said, stepping past him and leaving the conservatory. "I have a job to finish."

CHAPTER THIRTY

One year ago…

Drake's phone buzzed in his pocket. He pretended to not notice Elise's subtle eye roll as he put the menu down and pulled it out to read the incoming message. Even on a date, Drake wasn't one to ignore a text or a call. He never knew if there was a fire at the company that needed to be put out, especially when it came to Edmund.

When he saw who the message was from, he frowned down at the two simple words:

I'm outside.

"Excuse me a minute," Drake said, rising from the table. "Order us a bottle of wine, and I'll be right back."

He ignored the quizzical look Elise gave him and hurried out of the restaurant. He walked a few feet down the block and found Cecily waiting at the corner. Compared to him in his dark, tailored designer suit, she was dressed casually in jeans, a black snug t-shirt and a waist-length leather jacket. The boots she wore echoed along the semi-quiet street as she walked up to meet him.

"I'm sorry to interrupt your date," she said.

"Can't this wait?" He asked.

"Not after the voicemail you left me. Tell me what's going on."

Drake sighed and put his back up against the brick wall of the restaurant and slid his hands into his pockets.

"He got to you, didn't he?" She asked.

"He's my brother."

She shook her head, obviously frustrated with him. "We already went over this, Drake. You agreed to help me find that money which is actually your family's money. Don't you care that he's stealing from your family, too?"

"Of course, I do."

"Then why the change of heart? I can get that money back for you."

He glared at her. "And how much of it do you want? What's your finder's fee?"

"Are you serious?"

He came away from the wall and stepped up close to her. "You seem to take too much of an interest in this money and in my family. What's your angle?"

She hesitated before confessing. "I believe someone in your family is working with Edmund."

Drake bellowed a derisive laugh. "That's ridiculous."

"Leo wants to follow in Edmund's footsteps, and Gianna was married to Edmund. Who's to say one of them isn't Edmund's partner?"

He was having a hard time tamping down the anger that threatened to boil over. He was brought up to always protect his family, and this woman who both infuriated and aroused him was threatening to go after them.

"You're barking up the wrong tree, Cecily."

She didn't back down. "What about your father? He may be retired from the business, but a titan like him still keeps himself abreast of what's going on."

He gripped her by the shoulders, turned her around and backed her into the brick wall. He leaned in so close their noses were practically touching.

"Stay away from my family. Do you understand me?"

"I want Edmund, his partner, and that money," she said, refusing to cower.

"Not at the expense of dragging my family's name through the mud or throwing suspicion on any of them. I gave you access to the corporate financials, so find your answers there."

"Haven't you learned your lesson yet? Edmund was family and didn't have a problem stealing from the company. Don't blame me because you can't trust the people in your own house."

"That's right. I have loyalty towards them because they're my family. That may be hard for you to understand because you grew up without one!"

The moment he said the words, he regretted them.

Her eyes widened in surprise and then narrowed in suspicion. "How do you know that?"

He didn't answer, and she shoved him away from her. "You did a background check on me?"

His silence was answer enough. He had an investigator send him a report about her, but it's what he did for anyone he was working with. But he never intended to use what he found against her.

She shook her head in anger and then waved a hand for him to go away. "Get back to your date. We'll talk soon."

Although he was still fuming, he knew the right thing to do would be to apologize. He started to come forward. "Look, Cecily I—"

"Just go," she snapped.

When he didn't move, she whispered a string of curses, turned and marched off. He continued to stand there and watch her as she walked away. When she was at the end of the block, she turned around and saw that he was still watching her. She shook her head again, quickened her pace and practically ran from him and what he knew about her.

"Drake?"

He turned to find that Elise had walked up behind him.

"Is everything all right?" She asked.

"Yeah, everything's fine." He quickly took one last glance at Cecily who was barely noticeable as she got farther away down the street.

"Who was that?" Elise asked.

He searched his mind for a lie. He could say she was one of his assistants, but instead went with a simple answer.

"It was nobody."

Elise chuckled. "From what I saw, she didn't look like nobody."

"Let's go inside," he said.

Drake put his hand on Elise's waist and turned her around to the restaurant, trying to rid his mind of Cecily. Elise was right. She wasn't just a nobody—not with how close he'd held her to him. He'd been so close, he could see the exact moment her brown eyes went from hostile to vulnerable.

CHAPTER THIRTY-ONE

The underground parking lot echoed with the hum of distant engines and the faint drip of water from a leaking ceiling. Faint yellow lights dimly illuminated the grimy concrete floor, casting shadows where vehicles sat.

In one of the more discreet corners, Leo sat in his sleek black sports car, his fingers drumming impatiently on the leather steering wheel and the throbbing bass of hip hop music doing little to distract him.

He glanced at the clock on the dashboard. Cole was late. Leo sighed, shifting in his seat to peer out the tinted windows into the dim corners of the garage, searching for any sign of Cole's nondescript sedan.

This waiting was unbearable. Ever since he found out Drake lied about knowing Cecily for over a year, he'd been chomping at the bit to find out more. Cecily was clearly up to something, worming her way into the family under false pretenses. Drake may have been blinded by lust for his new wife, but Leo's eyes were wide open. He was on a mission to find out anything that would take Drake out of the CEO seat and sit himself in it. But first, he needed ammunition, and he was counting on Cole to give it to him.

A light knock on the window surprised him. It was Cole. Leo lowered the volume of the music and quickly unlocked the door, allowing him to slip into the plush leather passenger seat.

"What did you find out?" Leo's voice was tight, almost strangled by anticipation.

Cole handed over a brown envelope. "Like I said, your brother already had me investigate her. She was orphaned at a young age and raised by the system until she was eighteen. She then joined the Air Force and used her GI Bill to go to college for forensic accounting. No criminal record. As far as dirt goes, there's not much here."

Leo rifled through the contents, hoping to find something that Cole might have missed. But there wasn't much, and a twinge of disappointment and frustration bit into him.

"I'm sure she's hiding something."

Cole cleared his throat, his expression uneasy. "She may be, but to be honest, Mr. Morgan, she's not who you should be worried about."

Leo turned to him, his eyes narrowing. "What do you mean?"

Cole hesitated, then drew out a photograph from his coat pocket and handed it over. It was a black and white snapshot of a café scene. In it, Gianna sat opposite a man, leaning in close with her expression one of deep concentration. The man, however, sent shivers down Leo's spine.

"I know this man," he said.

"Tony Green," Cole murmured.

"Edmund put a price on his head before he died," Leo said. "But he never told me why he wanted him taken out."

"Tony was working for the company, but Edmund found out he was stealing from him," Cole supplied. "In my line of work, it's dangerous to jump to conclusions, but I'm wondering if Gianna was working with him to steal from Edmund and your company."

Leo's fingers tightened around the photo as his mind raced. Despite his resentment toward Gianna for her brief mourning of Edmund, he never believed she was a crook. Who was Tony Green to her? Were they lovers? Was Cole right and she was collaborating with him to siphon off the family money?

"Does Drake know about this?" Leo asked.

Cole shook his head. "I just found this out myself, but when you called, I decided to come to you first. Your brother is my next call."

"No. Don't tell him anything. He should hear this from me. For now, I want everything you can find on Tony Green. And keep an eye on Gianna. I need to know her next move."

Cole nodded. "Will do. Just be careful, Leo. If Gianna is involved with Tony, this could get messy. And the last thing your family and company needs is another scandal."

With that, Cole slipped out of the car and disappeared into the shadows of the underground garage. Leo stayed put, lost in thought with the photograph still clutched in his hand. He hated to think that he'd been wasting his time chasing after Cecily when who he should've been concerned about were the enemies in his own home.

CHAPTER THIRTY-TWO

Cecily sat back in the desk chair feeling both amazement and disbelief. There it was in black and white. After months of searching, the name of Edmund's partner stared back at her from the glowing screen of her laptop. She had to give respect to Drake and Leo's late brother—he'd covered his tracks well. If he hadn't been a crook, he would've made an excellent forensic accountant. Then again, considering who his partner was, she understood why he'd gone to such great lengths to suppress the name. He was a thief protecting those he loved.

She tore her eyes from the screen, pulled out her cell and sent a quick text to Tony.

Cecily: I'm on my way to see you now.

"You know that you and I are the only ones left in the building except for the front desk security and the cleaning crew."

Cecily practically jumped out of her seat at the sound of Drake's voice. She discreetly slipped her phone into her pocket and looked at him, trying not to give away the bombshell she had just discovered.

"Everything okay?" Drake asked, stepping into her office that she lovingly nicknamed "the broom closet."

She quickly closed the lid of her laptop and stood. "Yeah, I'm good. I have an excuse for being here late. What's yours?"

"There's some property I've been interested in buying, and the seller is giving me a run for my money."

"I'm sure you can afford it," she said, and stood to begin gathering her things. "Listen, I have an errand I need to run, so I'll be a little late getting home."

She needed to see Tony immediately and tell him she had found the account. She couldn't wait to see his face when he realized he could get his life and reputation back. After over a year, it was finally over.

"Whatever it is, cancel it. You're coming with me."

"Drake, I can't," she said, hoping he didn't hear the panic in her voice.

"Yes, you can. I have a chopper waiting on the roof."

Her hands went to her hips. "A chopper? What's going on?"

"What's going on is I made plans for us."

She started to argue, but he cut her off.

"Look Cecily, I'm trying to escape from the world for just a few hours, and I'd like it if you would escape with me. Whatever it is, can't it hold for tonight?"

She wanted to refuse, but the truth was, after what she found, a temporary escape sounded heavenly, and a few more hours wouldn't hurt anything.

She hesitated a beat longer and then expelled a deep breath and nodded. "Yeah, it can wait."

They took the elevator up to the roof where a helicopter was indeed waiting. The pilot secured her laptop bag and purse, and Drake helped her inside. He boarded after her, and they donned their headgear before the pilot took off.

As they were lifted into the evening sky, she welcomed the beautiful sights as they soared over San Francisco. As the world rapidly shrank beneath them and they headed north out of the city, she admired landmarks she'd come to take for granted from the years she'd been living there. From Coit Tower to the Golden Gate Bridge—it all now looked so beautiful to her. She turned and saw that Drake was watching her admire the city with awe, and she smiled with embarrassment.

"Are you going to tell me where we're going?" She asked.

He gave her a wicked smile. "I'm cashing in my raincheck."

* * *

It took nearly no time before the waters of San Francisco Bay turned into the blue waters of the Pacific Ocean, and they were soaring over the shores of Stinson beach. Cecily shook her head in wonderment when the chopper landed on a helipad in the back of Drake's beach house in Stinson.

"You know we could have just driven here," she said, laughing.

"The last time you drove here, you complained about the traffic," he said. "I thought tonight I'd spare you all that. Come on."

When the blades powered down, he got out and extended his hand for her. Together, they walked across the lawn to the two-story beach house that sat perched and regal on a cliffside overlooking the Pacific. She stepped onto the deck of the house, and then paused and leaned against the weathered railing, closing her eyes as the sea salt air caressed her face.

"How do you not come out here more often?" She asked.

"Running a company takes a lot of my time," Drake said, coming to stand beside her.

"You should make time for this."

"Dinner's almost ready, but we can wait in the living area for now," Drake said and led her inside to a large room just off the dining room.

The living area housed floor-to-ceiling windows and an unencumbered view of the ocean. The afternoon sun was quickly dipping below the horizon. Soon, there would be nothing to see but darkness, but the crashing waves would still be heard.

"You seemed really focused on your work," he said, handing her a glass of wine from the minibar. "Did you find anything new?"

"No," she hedged. "But I'm getting close."

He reached out to caress her face. "If there was something I needed to know, you'd tell me, wouldn't you?"

She stepped out of his reach, afraid that if she let him touch her, she'd lose focus on the endgame. She'd found what she and Tony had been after. That's what was important. Still, she thought that maybe she owed Drake something, considering she'd invaded his life and his home for months. But telling him what she knew would only jeopardize everything.

"Mr. Morgan?"

They both turned to see his chef smiling at them. "Dinner is served."

"Thank you, Tom. We'll be all right for the rest of the evening," Drake said. "Can I have my driver take you home?"

"No, thank you, Mr. Morgan, I'll be fine. Have a good evening. You too, Mrs. Morgan."

"Thank you," Cecily said, not sure if she'll ever get used to hearing herself referred to as Drake's wife.

He escorted her into the dining room and pulled a chair out for her. The course started with beluga caviar, followed by a summer truffle salad and ended with the entrée, an oysters and mussels dish in champagne and saffron broth.

Cecily inhaled the scents with an eager smile as Drake topped off her wine and then took the seat across from her.

"This smells delicious," she said.

"It tastes even better," he said with a wink.

They sat in silence for a moment as she savored her meal.

"Tell me something about yourself," he said.

She chewed and swallowed her food then took a sip of her wine.

"Didn't your investigators tell you everything you needed to know about me?"

"Touché," he said with a smile. "But those are just the basics that anyone could find out. Tell me something I don't know, and I already know you paint as a hobby, so that doesn't count."

She stared at him across the table, studying him, wondering just how much she could trust him. After what she found out this evening, she wasn't sure if he was an ally or an enemy. But like in Houston, it was just the two of them here alone, and for once, she was going to shut away the outside world, take a chance and allow him to see a minuscule of her heart.

"My parents died when I was ten."

"From a car accident," he finished. "I know that, and I'm sorry."

"But you don't know that it was my fault."

He leaned forward in his chair, placing his elbows on the table and intertwining his fingers together. He didn't move or make a sound but continued to stare at her, patiently waiting for her to get it out.

"Every summer, we'd pack the car up and drive from Arizona to California and spend a few days at a motor lodge near the beach. It was our yearly family vacation. We'd spend hours on the beach; my mom would splash and swim in the water, my dad would read his latest thriller, and I would sketch the ocean." She paused with a faint smile. "It wasn't until later that I started to paint."

"Anyway, for years, they had been promising me a trip to Disneyland and the year I turned ten, we were finally going. Unfortunately, the school they were teaching at went through a round of budget cuts and just like that, they'd lost their jobs, and our trip was cancelled."

"I could've been more understanding, but like the child I was, I threw a fit that I wasn't going to be able to go to Disneyland. I accused them both of never keeping their promises, which wasn't true at all. They left me with a sitter while they attended a school faculty meeting that evening to see what could be done, if anything, about their jobs."

She paused to look down at her plate, replaying the memories in her head. "That was the last time I saw them."

Silence reigned for several moments in the dining hall before Drake spoke up.

"There's no way that you're to blame for that."

She shrugged. "They were already upset to have lost their teaching jobs and add to that, their daughter tells them she hates them both. No wonder my father didn't see the delivery truck."

"Cecily—"

"I don't even know where they're buried," she said, gulping down the rest of her wine and trying her best to not break down. "I never bothered to find out."

"It must've been hard to be a ward of the State for all those years."

"Believe it or not, one of my foster parents were very

interested in adopting me. I knew this, and I liked them too, but I felt as if I were betraying my parents if I got a new family. So, I behaved like a brat, hoping it would change their minds."

"Where'd you get that?"

She looked up and realized he was gesturing to her necklace, which she had a habit of fiddling with whenever she talked about her past.

"It was a gift. I've had it for years."

"It's a white opal, right?" He asked.

She nodded and tucked the necklace back inside her shirt. "My birthstone."

She noticed Drake's features turn sorrowful, which is why she never talked about her parents. She didn't want his pity because if he knew the whole truth, he'd see she didn't deserve an ounce of it. Not really.

"Your turn," she said, slamming the door on her past. "Tell me something about yourself that I don't know."

He looked as if he would try to get her to continue talking, but let it go and rose from the table.

"First, let me show you my favorite room in the house, the master suite."

Cecily slowly stood and sent him a look filled with suspicion.

"It's not what you think," he said, laughing. "I love that room for a completely different reason than the obvious, but we need to hurry before the sun sets."

He led her upstairs where there were several guest rooms. At the top of the landing, they turned a corner, went down a long hallway and came to a pair of closed double doors. Drake used both hands to open the doors and stepped back.

Nothing but ocean stared back at Cecily as she stepped into the room. More floor-to-ceiling windows spanned the length of one wall and French doors led to a private deck outside. At the center of it all was a bed big enough for a family of five.

"It's gorgeous," she said, standing before one of the windows by the bed and watching the sun turn a fiery orange hue. "I would love to paint this."

"Just listen," Drake said, coming to stand behind her.

Together, they stood there in silence listening to the waves crashing. Cecily imagined sleeping here at night with nothing but the sound of the water lulling her to dreamland. She realized at that moment why she loved those summer trips to the beach as a child and why she chose California as her home. She wanted to be near the ocean because it represented everything she longed for her own life to be—free, passionate, and alive.

"My family has done some terrible things," Drake said, his voice strained with emotion. "Things I'm not proud of."

"I did my research," she said, keeping her eyes on the view.

"When you saw me in Houston, I was thinking about not coming back. I was going to take the jet somewhere far away where no one knew me. I wanted to escape it all."

"That's what I was afraid of," she said, "and that's why I followed you. I had to convince you to come back. Not for myself, but for your family and your company."

"Why? After everything I did to my own brother, what kind of leader am I?"

She turned to look at him. "Why do you do that? Why do you doubt yourself? You're not the kind of CEO people barely see. You walk up and down the halls, getting to know everyone in all the departments. I hear whispers, and they all respect you. They see that you're committed to changing the way things were run under Edmund. With him, it was tyrannical, but with you, it's productive and peaceful. You're the leader they need."

Gratitude filled his eyes. "Thank you."

She nodded and started to bring a hand up to caress his face and then paused, reminding herself she couldn't afford to get lost in this tender moment with him. She turned her back to him and once again faced the ocean view.

"Why did you bring me here, Drake?" She asked.

He wrapped his hands around her waist and brought himself close to her. His touch was electric.

"To get you alone."

"Why?"

"Remember our talk about secrets in Vegas? You are your own secret, and you only show your true self to me when no one's around."

He kept one hand clutching her waist, while the other slowly dipped lower and inside her pants. She should stop him, but her breath began to grow shallow with excitement, anticipating the moment he would find her center.

"No one can find us here." He began to kiss her neck and gently bite her earlobe. "Now, show me the woman you love to keep hidden."

The ringtone of Cecily's phone sounded inside her pocket.

"Let it ring," he said and began to let his fingers dance inside her panties.

"They'll just keep calling," she said, huskily.

"You can answer it when you let that woman out."

She lifted her arms and reached behind her to cradle his neck. Drake's hand cupped her, and she moaned, moving her ass against him and feeling him go rigid. When her phone sounded again, he reached his free hand into her pocket and pulled it out. They both saw the brightly lit display that read *Tony*.

"Should I answer it?"

Cecily closed her eyes, unable to think. His fingers were relentless as they played with her.

"You want him to hear you come?"

"Drake," she moaned.

"Is that a yes?"

She shook her head to clear the haze of sexual excitement and tried grabbing for the phone. But he moved it out of her reach while his fingers circled and rubbed her wetness.

"Let me see her, Cecily," he demanded. "Let me see the woman you keep a secret."

Knowing she was powerless, she stopped her attempt to grab the phone and tended to her waiting orgasm. She plunged one of her hands into her slacks and urged his fingers on.

What if someone walked by? What if someone saw them in the window?

"Jesus," Drake groaned. "You just got wetter. What are you thinking about?"

She turned her face up to look at him and forced his head down to kiss her. Instantly, she heard the sound of her phone fall to the floor as he placed all of his attention on her. He had both of his hands inside her—one to tease and one to plunge. The alternating sensations made her go crazy with wanting, and before she could stop it, she was moaning and screaming into his mouth as her orgasm overpowered and exploded from within her.

When her muffled cries subsided, Drake removed his hands from her slacks and wrapped his arms around her waist, holding her to him while she regained her breath.

Her phone rang at her feet. She looked down at the display and saw it was Tony again.

"Christ," she muttered, bending down to pick up the phone. "I need to get back to the city."

He frowned. "What's so important?"

"I just need to get back to work," she said, pulling away from him and straightening her clothes. "We can't do this."

"You've been saying that since Houston."

She sighed and looked at him with exasperation. "Well, maybe I need to keep saying it until you hear me or until I hear myself."

"Why?" He asked. "What would be so wrong about you and I making love and…"

"And what?" She asked. "Going on dates to expensive and exclusive restaurants? Taking exotic trips to faraway places in your private jet? Having a relationship?"

He shrugged. "Sure. Why not?"

"Because it's ridiculous. Because it would never work for the simple fact of who you are and who I am. Not to mention, it compromises everything."

"Compromises what?" He asked. We're on the same side here. We want the same thing."

She glared at him. "Do we?"

He frowned and she knew he was trying to read her thoughts. "What's wrong?"

"Have you told me everything, Drake?"

"Damn right, I have," he said. "I've been nothing but honest with you. It's you that's holding back."

"What do you mean?"

"Tell me how you feel about me. Tell me you want me just as much as I want you. We've been in each other's lives for over a year and from day one, I've wanted you. Tell me it wasn't the same for you."

She threw up her arms. "I can't go down that road with you."

"What are you scared of? What do you think is going to happen?"

She didn't say anything because the answer would show him just how vulnerable she felt around him and how much she thought of what could've been if things had been different.

"I need to go," she said, again.

The moment of escape was over. It was time to return to the world and confront what was waiting for her.

CHAPTER THIRTY-THREE

"Come in." Tony greeted Cecily with a warm smile and invited her inside the apartment. "I was expecting you sooner. Your text sounded urgent."

"Yeah, sorry," she said, her mind zooming to Drake, the oysters, his beach house, and his fingers inside her panties. "I got held up."

"Have a seat," he said. "Can I get you something to drink?"

"No, thank you. I'm not staying long. I just wanted to give you this."

He frowned at the thumb drive she held out, took it from her and thumped it along his palm.

"Is this what I think it is?"

She didn't say anything, but the look in her eyes told him all he needed. He went to the card table in the corner of the living room where his laptop sat open. He inserted the thumb drive, and it didn't take long before the figures, spreadsheets and charts filled the screen. It only took him a few minutes to decipher it all, and by the time he finished, he was beaming from ear to ear.

He glanced her way, unable to contain his excitement. "You found the account."

"I did," she confirmed.

He couldn't hold it back any longer. He slapped a hand down on the table in joy. "Fuck yeah, Cee!"

He closed the distance between them, scooped her up into his arms and held her tight. "I knew you were the right one for the job."

He spun her around, whooping and hollering and then put her down and framed her face with his hands.

"You're fucking brilliant!"

What he did next surprised them both. He probably hadn't expected to kiss her, but she chalked it up to him being so overcome with joy and gratitude.

After several moments of reacquainting herself with his lips and even relived memories of her body beneath him, guilt washed over her as Drake entered her thoughts. She ended the kiss and pulled away from him.

"Thanks," she said.

She put distance between them, and it was then that he seemed to really study her.

"Are you all right? You don't look too happy about this. It's over. We're done."

"I'm fine," she said, but her voice sounded unconvincing even to her. "I just didn't expect..."

"You didn't expect it to be Drake," Tony finished for her.

She nodded. "Doesn't it seem just a little too convenient? Edmund dies leaving evidence that his brother is an embezzler?"

Tony shrugged. "Sounds about right to me. That whole family has a shady past. I told you not to underestimate Drake Morgan. He may act as though he's trying to be a boy scout, but his hands are just as dirty as his brothers'. Now, thanks to you, we can nail his coffin and ship it."

"But...what if he didn't know about it?" She asked, still feeling uncertain about this whole thing.

"What the hell is wrong with you?"

"I just want to be sure this is solid before we—"

"Knowing you, I'm sure you vetted the information three times before bringing it to me," he said. "Is it legit?"

She hesitated before nodding. "Yeah."

"Then you've done your job."

Cecily nodded again. She had checked the data over and over in hopes she'd been wrong. She'd hoped it was all fabricated. But the truth was in the financials. Edmund had named Drake as an authorized user in the account that held hundreds of millions of stolen company profits. No matter how much she wanted to deny it, Drake was Edmund's partner.

She sighed heavily. "You're right."

"I know I'm right. Now get going. I have a lot of calls to make before we end this."

He fished his cell phone from his back pocket and then frowned when he saw that she hadn't moved.

"What's wrong?" He asked.

"Why were you in Houston?"

He challenged her stare and then looked down at his phone and slowly put it away.

"I followed Drake to make sure he wouldn't disappear," she said. "Now, I come to find out that you were on that same plane. You followed me."

"I did," he confessed.

"Why?"

"I told you before I was starting to question whether you had the stomach to see this through."

She scoffed. "But that was months ago. You were doubting me even back then?"

"Yeah."

"Why? What reason have I ever given you to think I couldn't do my job?"

He sighed. "As much as you try to hide it, I can see you have a soft spot for him. I see it right now, and I knew eventually it would affect your judgment when it came to him."

"I found the account and the account holder, didn't I?"

"Yes, you did, and I can only imagine how hard it was for you to bring this to me, especially after you slept with him."

Her eyes widened. "How did you know?"

He shrugged. "I didn't know for sure until now."

Silence lay between them like a gauntlet before Tony sighed again.

"Look, Cee, I honestly don't give a shit. You want to have some fun on the side, that's your business. No matter your poor judgment, you got the job done, and that's all that matters. No one will hear anything else from me."

She was at a loss for words and simply turned to leave.

"Don't beat yourself up," Tony said. "This is a big win for us, and you should be proud of yourself for that."

She forced a smile. "Yeah. A big win."

* * *

As soon as Cecily closed the door behind her, Tony mentally counted to twenty and then went to the door and opened it. The stairwell smelled old and musty, but it was nevertheless empty.

He closed the door, pulled his cell from his back pocket and scrolled to the first number in his contacts. When the line was answered, he wasted no time in getting to the point.

"I have the account," he said, his voice low and urgent. "Let's move forward now."

"Finally," the caller said.

"And you'll never believe whose name is on the account right next to Edmund's."

"Who?"

"Drake."

Silence fell on the other end. "Edmund's partner was Drake?"

"It looks that way."

More silence.

"Are you there?" Tony asked.

"Yeah, I'm just surprised. He's not who I expected."

Tony shrugged. "Edmund knew how to manage risk, and Drake would've been the least risk. If anything happened to Edmund, they probably planned for Drake to always take over as CEO and keep access to the offshore money."

"So, what now?"

"We stick to the plan," Tony said, feeling relief and triumph wash over him.

This had been going on for too long that he thought he'd never find that account. He didn't think he'd ever retrace Edmund's steps because the bastard was that damn cunning. But he'd beat him, and it was all thanks to Cecily.

CHAPTER THIRTY-FOUR

rake tried concentrating on the contract for the land acquisition his realtor had sent over, but he couldn't keep his mind focused on anything. He picked up his phone for what must've been the hundredth time and cursed when he didn't see a text, voice message or missed call from her. He pressed the phone icon and dialed her number.

"You've reached Cecily Reed. Please leave your name, number and a brief message at the tone..."

Goddammit. He ended the call without leaving a message and put the phone down. Where the hell could she be? After they returned to the city last night, they went their separate ways as if nothing had happened which pissed him off so much, he couldn't concentrate on anything the rest of the evening. When she finally returned to the mansion at nearly eleven at night, he was waiting in the study for her. She must've seen the dim lamplight and just as he'd hoped, she stepped inside to find him sitting in a club chair by the fire.

* * *

"Did you finish your errand?" He asked.

"I did," she said, taking her jacket off. "I just came in to say goodnight and to thank you for dinner."

He nodded, trying to keep his temper in check. He didn't want her thanks. He wanted her.

"I hope Tony wasn't too upset that you made him wait."

"He just wanted an update on how things were going. I gave it to him and left." She paused. "It's what I've always done, Drake. Nothing more."

"And what is the update?"

She moved from one foot to the other, and it occurred to him that it was the first time he'd ever seen her nervous.

"That I'm close to finding the account. I'll be out of your life soon. Goodnight."

He nodded and spoke somberly as she headed for the door. "So, it won't be long now."

"I'm sure Elise will be pleased," she said under her breath.

She was at the door when she made that parting shot, and it ignited something within him. Drake shot up from the chair and got to the door before she could make a cowardly escape. He then grasped her shoulders, turned her around, and brought her up hard against his body.

"Damn you!" He cursed, his eyes and entire stature blazing with fury. "I've known her for years, but she could never affect me as much as you have in the short time we've known each other. No, I may not love her, but she never lied to me, extorted a marriage out of me or convince me to turn on my family."

"You could've said no," she said. "I'm just doing my job!"

"For him! You're doing all this for him," he accused. "Do you know what it does to me to know that you'll never go as far for me as you do for him? I kissed you, felt what it was like to be inside you, and I still can't get to your heart like he has."

They were both breathing heavily now, confronted by the truth in his words. Then Drake's eyes dipped to her mouth, which she parted just slightly enough to welcome him.

"I'll take what I can get," he hissed and in the next second, he was devouring her.

At first, the kiss was fast and hard as his lips moved over hers. He needed to claim her, possess her, and make her his. Then he slowed down, and his lips turned soft, seeking and wanting.

Cecily raised her arms, and he pulled her shirt up, off her head and tossed it to the side. She unhooked her bra and flung it away then wrapped her arms around his neck, crushing him to her with a deeper kiss. Drake emitted a low growl and led her over to the sofa.

"Turn around," he ordered.

She did so, and he immediately bent her over the back of it. Drake unzipped his pants and Cecily shimmied out of her jeans and panties. He caressed her ass and leaned down and planted tender kisses along the curve of her spine before plunging himself into her. They moaned and called and cried out for each other as he moved in and out of her with abandon, both reaching for that same shattering climax.

* * *

"I can hear you thinking."

They were lying on the floor in front of the fireplace covered by two wool throws. Cecily lay with her forearm over her head and stared up at the ceiling while Drake lazily fiddled with the opal necklace resting between her breasts. His eyes slowly trailed to her deep brown nipples that were just barely peeking out over one of the throws and tempting the hell out of him.

When she didn't answer, he brought his gaze up to her

eyes. "Is this the part where you tell me this can't happen again?"

She turned to her side to face him. "Is there anything you want to tell me? Anything at all?"

He shook his head. "No."

But the look in her eyes told him she wasn't satisfied with his answer. Drake sighed and reached out to tuck a strand of hair behind her ear.

"I asked you before, and you avoided the question, so I'm going to ask you again. Is there anything I need to know?"

She closed her eyes looking weary. "No, nothing. It's been a long day, and I'm just exhausted."

"Stay with me tonight."

He hadn't planned to say that, but it's what he'd desired for months now. They'd had mind-blowing sex but had yet to sleep in the same bed and wake up to each other in the morning.

But his hopes were instantly dashed when he saw the refusal on her lips before she spoke one word.

"I don't think that's a good idea. Have your lawyer draw up the annulment papers. This arrangement is over, Drake."

A slew of curses went through his mind. In a flash, he rose from the floor and grabbed his trousers and shirt. He slipped the trousers on without a word, shrugged on his shirt and didn't bother buttoning it. He then stood by the study door, to wait for her. When she was dressed, she met him at the door and paused. She pulled the wedding ring he'd given her from her left finger and handed it to him.

"You should have this back," she said. "It was just loaner after all."

He snatched it and tucked it in his pocket. He then took her face between his hands and searched her eyes for any sign that she didn't want him to walk out of her life. But there was nothing there. He let her go, and she brushed by him, leaving the scent of her fragrance in her wake.

When he heard her soft steps mounting the staircase to her bedroom, he told himself to not go after her. Instead, he remained in the study alone, cursing himself for wanting her so much. He then cursed whoever or whatever convinced her she didn't deserve to be happy.

* * *

By the time Drake had come downstairs for breakfast the next morning, Cecily was gone. His father said she'd only grabbed a cup of yogurt for breakfast and had left. She hadn't come into the office, and he even called the recreation center to see if she was there. They hadn't seen her either. He would've been worried, but she'd managed to send him one text saying she was just incredibly busy and would see him tonight.

Now, it was nearing eight o'clock, and he'd skipped dinner, wondering about her absence. Gianna had the house-keeper bring him a tray in the study, but he hadn't touched his food. He knew Cecily was avoiding him, but he didn't know why, and the moment she walked in the door or answered her damn phone, he was going to ask her.

Out of the corner of his eye, he saw red and blue strobe lights flash outside the study window. Frowning, Drake rose from the desk and crossed the room to pull the drapes aside and look outside. Several cop cars and unmarked federal vehicles surrounded the driveway. Seconds later, a loud pounding sounded at the front door.

"What the hell is going on?" He heard Leo asking just outside the study.

Drake opened the double doors to the study and stepped out to see Leo and Gianna following the housekeeper to the front door. As soon as she opened it, a team of cops and federal officers swarmed the foyer, announcing themselves as FBI and SFPD.

"Excuse me," Leo said, his voice rising above the uproar. "You have no right to enter this home without a warrant."

But Drake ignored his brother's words and focused on each individual agent entering his home until he saw the one he was waiting for, trailing the pack.

Last night, her hair was free and loose, her eyes had been closed and her mouth opened in ecstasy as he fingered her to orgasm at the beach house; and the second time, when he had her just a few feet away bent over the sofa and calling out his name. Tonight, however, her hair was styled in that customary French roll she preferred with her mouth closed and full lips pressed firmly together. Her eyes were open and searching the room until they found him, too. She moved through the team of law enforcement personnel and stopped as soon as she was directly in front of him.

"Please turn around and place your hands behind your back," Cecily said, quietly.

"You finally found it," he concluded, staring into her eyes and trying to see any remnant of the woman he'd been able to uncover.

"Turn around," she ordered.

They stared at each other as though it were just the two of them in the room. Finally, he slowly turned and put his hands behind his back. His gaze fell to his family who were staring back at him in shock.

"Don't put those cuffs on him," Ivan said, trying to come forward.

"It's all right, Dad," Drake said, forestalling him. "Let her do her job."

"Gianna, call Tara," Leo commanded. "She'll have the number to his attorney."

As Gianna rushed away, Drake felt the metal handcuffs go around his wrists, and the slight brush of Cecily's fingers was too much to bear. Then she was standing in front of him and the disappointment in her eyes wounded him.

"Just get it over with," he hissed to her.

She nodded. "Drake Morgan, you're under arrest for the charge of embezzlement. You have the right to remain silent."

CHAPTER THIRTY-FIVE

One year ago…

Drake stood on the weathered planks of the wharf, the salty breeze from the San Francisco Bay whispering through his hair. The city lights twinkled in the distance, casting a vibrant glow upon the water's surface. As he waited for her, his mind raced with conflicting thoughts and emotions. The loyalty he felt towards his family clashed with the truth he had been ignoring for too long—his brother, Edmund, needed to be stopped.

Soft steps along the wharf interrupted his thoughts, and Drake turned to find Cecily approaching, her silhouette framed against the backdrop of the night, and her gaze fixed upon him with unwavering determination. It startled him to realize he was instantly attracted to her, even as it fueled his resentment towards her.

"After we met at the restaurant, I was sure you'd call soon," she said and stopped just inches from him. "But as the days went by and no call from you, I was beginning to wonder if I had you pegged all wrong and that you were just like your brother."

The night air hung heavy with anticipation as Drake and Cecily stood in silence on the desolate wharf. The faint sound of the water lapping against wood pilings mingling with the distant hum of the city, created an eerie setting for their clandestine meeting.

Let's be clear," he said, his voice filled with bitterness for both himself and her. "I'm doing this for my family and the company, not for you. I don't trust you, especially since this is only a job for you."

Cecily met his gaze, her eyes reflecting the moonlight. "I understand, but for what it's worth, this isn't just a job to me."

"Yeah, whatever. So, what now?"

"You go back to work as COO as if everything were normal. You observe what you see and report to me and only me."

"How are you going to prove he's embezzling?"

"You let me worry about that."

He narrowed his eyes and stepped into her space. "Unacceptable. You're going to tell me your exact plan since it involves the company."

She frowned, seemingly offended by his tone. "Before this goes any further, let's set some ground rules. Rule number one, I'm in charge which means you're only privy to what I think you should know. This is my investigation, and you take orders from me."

"I don't take orders from anyone," he amended.

She glared at him but continued. "Rule number two, you discover anything, you call me, no matter how small or irrelevant you think it is. Let me be the judge of that."

Drake clenched his fists, feeling the tension course through his body. Her bossiness and take-charge attitude was alluring to him, but how could he be attracted to the woman who represented his own treachery against his brother?

She stepped closer to him, her expression now softening. "Look, I know this isn't easy for you. It takes great courage to stand against your own blood. But together, we can expose the truth and protect what your father built."

He scoffed. "Please stop acting as if you care one fucking ounce about me or my family."

She looked ready to argue but then gave a wan smile and reached out to shake his hand. "You'll be hearing from me. Good night, Mr. Morgan."

He looked at her hand, shook his head with bemusement and grasped it. "Good night, Agent Reed."

The moment their hands clasped, he felt something electric pass between them, and the way she was looking at him, he knew without a doubt that she felt it, too.

* * *

Cecily kept her face expressionless when she walked into the stark and sterile interview room and sat down at the metal table.

"Thank you for your patience, gentlemen."

"Are the handcuffs necessary, Agent Reed?" Drake's lawyer, Mr. Wilson asked. "As my client's wife, you could at least show him a little courtesy."

Her gaze flickered from Wilson to Drake. After a beat, she stood, removed the handcuff keys from her belt and freed Drake's wrists. But being close to him was a mistake. She couldn't help but inhale his cologne, which only brought memories of him covering her body with his, stroking in and out of her while she buried her face in his neck, allowing him to carry her away.

"Thank you," Drake said.

She didn't respond but moved to the other side of the table and took her seat again. She then opened the thick file folder before her.

"Mr. Morgan, we have evidence linking you to several offshore accounts that were used to siphon funds from Morgan Global Solutions."

"May I?" Wilson asked.

Cecily handed a sheet of paper to him that showed the account numbers and Drake's name as account holder. For the moment, she had to endure the silence while avoiding Drake's stare.

Wilson snorted derisively. "This is all circumstantial. There is no proof that my client set these accounts up on his own. Edmund, or anyone for that matter, could have added his name to the accounts. From what I understand, you had access to the company financials, Agent Reed."

Cecily saw red. "What are you insinuating?"

"I'm just pointing out the fact that anyone could've added Mr. Morgan's name to the accounts and how easy it would have been."

Her fists clenched. "I'm not setting him up."

"Well, you did blackmail him into a marriage, so you're just about capable of anything."

Before she could lay into him, Drake spoke up as he looked to his attorney.

"Leave us," he commanded.

Wilson turned to him in surprise. "Mr. Morgan, I advise you to just let me handle this."

"I said leave."

Cecily could feel Wilson brimming with indignation, and he looked as if he would challenge Drake. But after several tense moments, he finally stood and left them alone in the room. She didn't move or breathe until she heard the door open and then firmly close. Finally, she looked at Drake and let her anger overtake her.

"Is this the card you want to play? The reason I married you is to set you up? That's ridiculous!"

Drake shrugged with indifference. "I pay him a lot of money to build my defense. Some tactics I may not agree with, but I trust him to do his job."

She shook her head in wonder. "All this time. I gave you plenty of chances to tell me. Why didn't you?"

"Without admitting to anything, I didn't know I was named on that account," he said calmly.

"Bullshit!"

"If I'd known that evidence existed of me being an embezzler from my own company, do you think I'd ever let you find it?"

"You mean you'd get rid of the evidence or get rid of me?"

He leaned back, looking as though his patience had run out. "You're talking to me, Cecily."

"I'm talking to a Morgan, and you and I both know what that name implies."

"I'd never hurt you, and you can pretend like I'm some criminal, but deep down, you know otherwise."

"Okay, so maybe you aren't a murderer, but you are a thief."

"I'm not. I don't know why Edmund put me on those accounts with him. He didn't tell me anything about it. So how about we drop this circus act and you let me help you find out why."

She smiled sarcastically. "Thanks, but I can manage fine on my own."

"Yeah. You've been doing it your whole life."

Unwilling to let him have that, she rose out of her chair and leaned in. "You've been playing me for a fool this entire time, but no more. I've got you, Drake."

He looked at her with an intensity that made his green eyes burn. "Yeah, you do. More than you'll ever know."

She stepped back, not liking the meaning behind those words. They challenged each other for a few more minutes until the door swung open and Drake's attorney along with Cecily's boss, SAC Richard Santos stepped in.

"Mr. Morgan, you're free to go," Richard said.

"What?" Cecily asked in outrage. "What's going on? Sir, I have evidence of this man's involvement in embezzlement."

"What you have is circumstantial. Where is the concrete evidence, Agent Reed?" Wilson asked while gesturing for Drake to stand.

"Agent Green has the thumb drive. It shows deposits for over two years to the offshore account. Bring him in here. He's the one who called this in."

Richard peered at her in anger. "Are you serious?"

"Yes, I'm serious," Cecily said. "Bring him in here, now."

The room grew silent as her boss and Drake's lawyer regarded one another curiously. There was something going on and apparently, she was being left in the dark.

Growing tired of the silence, Cecily erupted with a shout. "What?"

Richard shook his head in disbelief. "Agent Green resigned from the bureau over a year ago."

When her mind processed the words, she still didn't believe them. "That can't be right."

"It's absolutely right," Wilson said. "Agent Green is probably halfway to Mexico by now with that stolen and proprietary account information. The methods you used to conduct your investigation were reckless, desperate and borderline entrapment. I plan to advise Mr. Morgan to file a civil suit against the agency and you personally, Agent Reed."

"That's enough, Fritz. You've made your point," Richard said. "Mr. Morgan, you're free to go with our apologies."

Drake hadn't said a word, but he kept his gaze on Cecily as his attorney led him out of the interview room. She watched them go, feeling as if over a year's worth of work was being flushed down the drain.

Once they were gone, she turned and pleaded with her superior.

"There's got to be some explanation. Sir, you have to believe me. I had no idea about Agent Green's status. He never told me he wasn't with the Bureau. He even led me to believe he was involved with this investigation."

"And you led me to believe you were acting alone," Richard countered. "If you had come to me and told me he put you up to this—"

"He told me no one at the Bureau would listen to him and asked me as a personal favor to keep it quiet," she said, hearing the desperation in her voice.

"Well, that personal favor may have cost you your job. You'll be brought up for discipline by the review board, and you'd better pray Drake Morgan doesn't follow through with his threat to sue, or you'll be out of the Bureau right along with Agent Green."

He opened the door to the interview room and paused to turn back to look at her.

"Or maybe that's what the two of you have been planning all along."

"What do you mean?" She asked.

"I'm not saying this is the case, but it would be very easy for you to find the account, orchestrate your termination, get fired and six months later, the two of you meet up in Argentina to split all that money."

Cecily shook her head in disbelief. "You know me better than that."

"I thought I did," Richard said. "Look, you want to save yourself? Tell me where Tony is now. Maybe we can stop him on his way out of town."

Cecily stared back, keeping her face stoic as she voiced the lie. "I have no idea."

He stormed out, leaving her alone. Cecily stared at the door and waited exactly sixty seconds before she slowly opened it, made sure no one was around and left the federal building, careful not to be seen.

CHAPTER THIRTY-SIX

Drake woke up early the next morning, the weight of the previous night's events heavy on his mind. After leaving the federal building downtown, he returned home in a daze. Thankfully, the entire house was silent, which saved him from having to explain how and why his wife put handcuffs on him. When he finally crawled into bed, he closed his eyes, but didn't really sleep. For the rest of the night, he tossed and turned restlessly, his mind replaying the accusations against him and the subsequent media frenzy that was sure to follow.

A few hours later, he dragged himself out of bed, his eyes bleary and sleep deprived. Nonetheless, he showered, shaved, and put on his best suit to prepare for the day. He'd already texted Tara to make sure his head of public relations was his first meeting of the morning. He'd yet to hear back from her but was confident she'd see to it.

On his way downstairs, he walked past Cecily's open bedroom door. He knew she wouldn't be in there, but he couldn't help but turn his head to look inside. She was gone, and she wasn't coming back.

"So, she's a Fed," Gianna said, coming up behind him.

He turned around to face her. "Yeah."

"Did you know?" She asked.

"Yes."

She let out a deep breath. "It all makes sense now. There was always this subtle hostility between you two which was so odd for two people just married. Then there was the heat."

"Gianna—"

"Don't forget that I walked in on the two of you in the conservatory. The staff and I all heard the raised voices one moment and then nothing. What you two have is electric." She paused and her features turned thoughtful. "I wish Edmund and I had that."

Drake allowed a moment of silence at the mention of his brother. He could say that if it wasn't for Edmund, he wouldn't be in any of this mess, but that wouldn't be fair to Gianna's memory of him.

He clutched her hand, leaned in and kissed her on the cheek. "I need to get to the office and do damage control."

* * *

The moment he arrived on the top floor of Morgan Global Solutions, he sensed something wasn't right. His suspicion heightened when he saw Tara standing just outside his office, looking uneasy. When he saw his security team packing his belongings into a box and setting aside company files, he knew instantly what was going on. But his heart refused to believe it.

"Mr. Morgan," Tara said, her eyes pleading with him and her voice shaking. "I wanted to call you, but your brother gave me strict orders to wait for you to come in."

"Where is he?"

"I'm right here," Leo said, stepping up to them, his expression grim. "Security downstairs told me when you arrived."

Drake whirled around to face him. "What are you doing, Leo?"

"Given last night's circumstances, I called an emergency meeting this morning with the board," he said. "We voted you out, Drake. You're no longer CEO of this company."

Drake simply stared at his brother, waiting for the fury to rise up within him. But surprisingly to himself, he remained calm and composed.

"You fired me?"

"I had to take steps. You were arrested for embezzlement. That's not the kind of news this company needs right now."

"Those charges were dropped. You didn't need to do this."

"The word is already out," Leo countered. "And whether the charges are dropped or not doesn't matter. The news of our CEO being arrested could've killed the IPO. We needed to act immediately."

Drake stepped up to him until they were toe to toe. "And I bet your first task as CEO was to call Gavin Reyes and finish the deal. Congratulations."

"After last night, you really think you deserve to be CEO?" Leo asked, his tone filled with ridicule. "You brought a Fed into our home and into our business without telling me."

"She wasn't after you."

"No, she was after Edmund, your brother and if he hadn't died, you would've served him up on a platter and slid into the CEO spot yourself."

"My duty has and always will be to this family and this business. Edmund was stealing from us, and I gave him a chance to resign with the money he stole. He refused, so I did what I had to do."

"You could've told me."

"You'd only defend him. I knew what I was doing."

"He was your brother," Leo accused.

Drake heaved a breath. "He was stealing from us. He was bringing the company down with his ruthless and dangerous tactics. We would've lost the company in a few years and probably would be in prison because of the destruction he was causing."

"So, you screwed him," Leo said.

"He did it to himself!"

"And it's because of you, he's dead. He found out what you were up to. That's why he was on that chopper."

Drake froze. "What are you talking about?"

"He found out you betrayed him and told me about it. He was boarding a chopper to get to the airport and get out of town. Our brother is dead because of you!"

Drake stepped back, his words failing him.

Leo took a moment to compose himself. "Look, just like you did what you had to do when it came to Edmund, I'm doing what I have to do for this company. We'll give you some time to clean out your office."

He didn't say anything more as he turned and headed down the hall to his office. Drake stared after him and then noticed the faces of the shocked and confused employees as they looked on. He went into his office, which was now cluttered with boxes and slammed the door.

He stood by the windows to look out at the city skyline and thought about his next move. He'd lost control of his company, and if it wasn't for his lawyer, he would've been headed to prison for embezzlement. Edmund had named him as an account holder. But why? Why would Edmund entrust him with his stolen funds knowing that it was just the proof Drake needed to give to the FBI?

Before parting ways last night, his lawyer had given Drake a copy of the bank statement from an account in the

Republic of Seychelles. His name was there beside Edmund's, which had given Cecily all she needed to arrest him. But as of last night, the hundreds of millions that had been in that account had been transferred out and the account closed. The FBI was certain their former agent, Tony Green, had done that and set up a new account under an alias.

Even worse, Wilson had informed Drake there was no sign of Cecily Reed. She hadn't returned to her condo last night, and there's suspicion that she and Tony Green hopped a plane out of town with the stolen money. Drake didn't want to believe that, but if it were true, he hadn't been married to an FBI agent at all. He'd been married to an Oscar-worthy actress and the world's best con artist.

A knock sounded and the door to his office swung open. Drake turned to see Tara standing there nervously.

"I'm sorry, Mr. Morgan, but these gentlemen need to continue packing up the office. Your brother gave explicit orders that it needed to be packed up today."

"Where's Cole?" Drake asked.

"He had a family emergency and took a personal day."

Drake racked his head for a solution. "Get me Walt's number."

"The private investigator?"

"Yeah. Tell him I need him to get me an address in Potrero Hill immediately."

"Yes, sir, but security is here to pack up your office."

Drake waved the men in who looked apologetic.

"Sorry, Mr. Morgan," one of them said.

"It's fine. Do what you have to do," he said and addressed Tara. "Call Walt now. I want that address in the next ten minutes."

CHAPTER THIRTY-SEVEN

She'd been hiding in his bedroom since last night. At first, she thought maybe she'd missed him, and he was halfway around the world by now. But as soon as she entered his apartment, she saw packed suitcases and realized he hadn't gone anywhere just yet. So, she hid in his closet and waited for the moment when he returned.

It was early the next morning when she finally heard his key turn in the lock and the front door open. She wondered where he'd been all night, but assumed he was making last-minute arrangements. After all, it took time to secure fake but genuine-looking passports, and he would need them to start a whole new life somewhere.

Cecily lied to her SAC about knowing where Tony was because there was no way in hell the FBI was going to get to him before she had her moment alone with him first.

From inside the closet, she could hear him moving about the apartment and his muffled voice as he spoke to someone on the phone.

"I've got the passports. Are you packed?" He asked. "I have

an Uber coming in fifteen minutes. We'll pick you up on the way to the airport. Yeah, see you soon."

When he hung up, Cecily emerged from the closet and made her way into the living room where he was flipping through a wad of money.

"You're not leaving without saying goodbye, are you?"

He whirled around, and as she'd anticipated, he drew his pistol from his waist. But by the time he turned, her gun was already up and aimed at his heart.

"Your locks are shit," she said.

He shrugged. "This place was never permanent. Just somewhere to hole up for a while."

"You mean, just long enough for me to do your dirty work for you."

She eyed his changed appearance. He'd dyed his hair and beard from dark brown to black.

"Do you think that'll be enough to fool the FBI? They have the airport surrounded."

"I'll take my chances. Do you want to talk?" He asked and took the gun off her and put it slowly down on the coffee table. He then held up his hands in surrender.

"Put the gun down, Cee."

She moved in closer, keeping the gun trained on him. "Don't call me that."

"We both know you're not going to shoot me," he said.

"Try me."

"Put the gun down, Agent Reed. Let's talk."

Several tense moments passed as they challenged each other in silence. Finally, she slowly put the gun down and when he visibly relaxed, she marched up to him and slapped him hard across the face.

"You son of a bitch," she screamed. "You fucking used me!"

He put a hand to the side of his face but stood there and took in her anger. "I'm sorry."

"You're sorry," she spat. "That's it? Fuck you, Tony. They're talking about firing me because of you."

"They won't fire you."

"Really? You're so sure about that?"

"I'm the one who's gone rogue with nearly half a billion dollars in an offshore account. They have enough to deal with."

"Money," she said. "This was all about money."

"Yeah. My fair share of money."

"Your fair share? What are you—" she paused and reacted when the answer slammed into her. "Jesus. You're Edmund's partner."

"Edmund never had a partner," he said. "I just knew he was stealing money, and I made a plan to relieve him of it. He added Drake as an authorized user in case anything happened to him."

"So, why did you need me?" She asked. "Why couldn't you just access the money on your own?"

"Because the son of a bitch found out I was a Fed. He was convinced I was there to take him down. So, he funneled the money through so many offshore accounts to the point where I couldn't find it and had his goons hunt me down like a dog. That's why I had to go into hiding."

"What about the FBI?"

"The SAC found out I was on an unsanctioned mission and that I failed to report the embezzlement. I was forced to resign, but they kept it quiet to avoid embarrassment to the agency. That's why you never heard about it."

"Why didn't you tell me?" Cecily asked.

He sighed. "We may have a history, but our relationship wasn't enough to remove your conscience. If I'd told you the truth, you never would've helped me. I had to lie to you."

He sounded so cold and dismissive, nothing like the man she remembered or the man she thought she was in love with.

He must have seen the hurt in her eyes because he made a hesitant step toward her and then another.

"Just stay where you are," she commanded.

He ignored the order and kept coming closer. "You loved me once, didn't you?"

"That was a long time ago."

"It wasn't that long ago."

He was upon her now and moved one hand slowly behind her neck to cradle it. He then leaned down and kissed her softly on the lips. Cecily allowed the feel of his lips to take her back to how things used to be, but the memories didn't last long because he wasn't the Tony she knew. He was a liar and a thief. She broke the kiss.

"Come with me," he said.

"You can't be serious."

The corner of his lips ticked up into a crooked smile. "Yeah, I know, but it couldn't hurt to ask."

She stared at him in sorrow. "You know I can't let you leave here."

He sighed and nodded. "I figured you wouldn't, which is why I wished you'd just stayed away."

Instantly, she felt the cold, hard press of metal against her abdomen.

Her heart raced as she stepped back, eyes wide. "Tony..."

"You say you know me so well, but you forgot I always carry an extra gun." His voice hardened. "Put your hands up and turn around and face the wall."

She hesitated but slowly raised her hands and eyed him with disdain before turning and facing the wall. Every second she had her back to him felt like an eternity. She listened to the rustle of fabric as he grabbed his backpack and duffel bag and finally his footsteps as he left the apartment and retreated down the stairs. Then came silence.

Just as Cecily lowered her hands and started to run after him, two gunshots pierced the air.

No! Immediately, her instincts kicked in. She pulled her gun from her waistband and burst out of the apartment. She descended the stairs two at a time. The sound of her shoes thudding against the wooden steps competed with her thudding heartbeat. Yet, the moment she hit the lobby, the sight before her stopped her dead in her tracks.

Tony was at the foot of the stairs, sprawled on the cold marble floor with blood quickly pooling around him. Movement out of the corner of her eye snagged her attention, and she looked up in time to see a shadowed figure darting away, escaping through the exit.

"Stop! FBI!" She yelled.

But just as she exited the apartment building, the figure vanished. With a surge of dread, Cecily raced back to Tony. She dropped to her knees. and felt for a pulse. Her fingers became slippery with his blood as she fumbled for her phone and dialed for an ambulance.

As she gave the dispatcher Tony's address, she rummaged through his backpack in search of anything that would tell her where he sent the money. But Tony wasn't stupid. He would've immediately transferred that money to his own account under an alias and hidden it away.

"Ma'am, the police and ambulance are on their way, just stay where you are," the dispatcher said.

But Cecily was barely listening as she came upon a folded newspaper clipping. She frowned as she unfolded it and saw a group posing for a photograph. She instantly recognized Tony standing to the far left in his Army Ranger uniform. The date of the clipping suggested this was from the days of his military time. Her gaze moved over the rest of the group, and her hands began to slightly shake the moment she noticed the person standing beside him. She looked to Tony and saw that he was now staring up at the ceiling. The light had gone out of his eyes just as the truth began to flood her thoughts.

CHAPTER THIRTY-EIGHT

*L*eo sat at the dimly lit bar of Salvador's, his eyes flickering between his watch and the door. He had been waiting for Drake for almost an hour, and his patience had deserted him. He took a sip of his whiskey, but it did little to calm his nerves.

He then put the glass down, pulled out his phone and dialed Drake's number. As it had done multiple other times, the call went straight to voicemail. Leo cursed under his breath and left a message, his voice tight with frustration.

"I told you to meet me at seven. I know you're pissed at me, but this is important. Get here now."

He hung up and took another sip of his drink and removed the photos Cole had given him that night in the underground parking lot from the inside of his jacket pocket and studied them again. This time, he focused solely on Gianna and something about her nagged at him. But he needed to speak to Drake to confirm that he wasn't crazy.

He hated to admit it, but he had come to rely on his brother's instincts and keen sense of awareness. In the face of chaos, Drake always seemed to know what to do. He maintained a sense of tranquility that was oddly comforting to Leo.

Removing him as CEO this morning had been a dick move, but he knew it was the right decision. Drake had been too distracted, too focused on his own interests instead of the company's. He'd brought a Fed into their lives, into their family, and he'd been too distracted by her beauty to not realize she had him in her crosshairs all along. Leo had gotten what he wanted—he'd stepped, took control and the power was all his. He tried to ignore the fact that it had come at a cost to his relationship with his brother, which had already been strained for years.

He waited a few more minutes, staring at the entrance to the bar and willing Drake to walk in. But it soon became clear that he wasn't coming.

"Fuck it," he muttered under his breath.

He sighed, signaled for the bartender and quickly settled his tab. He tucked the photos back into his jacket, got up from the barstool and made his way to the door. Drake had to come home at some point, or maybe he was hiding out at the beach house in Stinson. Leo decided he would just make the trip out there and make him listen.

He stepped out into the cool night air but didn't make it a few feet before he heard the sound of footsteps behind him. He turned, hoping it was Drake and that he'd put aside his anger and decided to come after all. But before he could react, he felt a searing pain rip into his skin, one, two, three times. He stumbled back and looked down in disbelief as blood stained his shirt. He tried to speak or call out, but his mouth was rapidly filling with the coppery taste of blood. The pain of being stabbed overwhelmed him, and he fell to the ground.

He lay on his back with his thoughts a jumble of confusion and fear. A shadow loomed over him, and he watched the eyes of his attacker staring down at him. The darkness obscured their features, but even as Leo's vision started to fade, he saw a black-gloved hand clutching a knife and the glint of the blade stained with his blood. He closed his eyes and took one last shuddering breath before everything went black.

CHAPTER THIRTY-NINE

One hour later…

Drake's heart raced as he pulled the car to the front entrance of UCSF Medical Center. He left it there, not giving a damn about tickets and tow fees, but got out and rushed through the doors into the hospital. When he got inside the elevator, his hands shook as he pressed the button for the floor where Gianna said she and Ivan were waiting. He exited onto the floor, ran down the hall and nearly plowed into Gianna as she was exiting the waiting room.

"Drake, he's all right," she rushed to say. "He's in surgery right now, but the doctors are optimistic."

Drake allowed the relief to wash over him as he allowed Gianna to lead him into the private waiting room and sit him beside Ivan who looked sullen. He clutched his father's hand, stared into space and shook his head as regret, guilt and shame weighed heavily on his shoulders.

"He wanted to meet me at Salvador's for drinks. He kept texting and calling, but I wouldn't respond to him. I was too angry."

"It's all right," Gianna said, soothingly.

"No, it's not all right," Ivan said, his voice booming in the silence. "This rivalry between you boys needs to stop. From my eldest son stealing from me, to you working with the FBI to turn him in, and Leo ousting you from the company…"

He released Drake's hold on his hand and pounded a fist on the armrest. "This is not how your mother and I raised the three of you. I'm disappointed in all of you."

"I'm sorry, Dad."

Drake looked from his father to Gianna. Her face was now flushed red and silent tears streamed down her cheeks.

"The police will be coming by to take our statements," she said. "Can you stay?"

"I'm not going anywhere," Drake said and pulled out his cell. "But I need to call Tara. She needs to get in touch with PR and get a statement prepared."

"Leo is CEO," Ivan said. "You need to call an emergency board meeting and get yourself reinstated."

"First Edmund, then me, then Leo and now back to me again," Drake said. "The flip-flopping is going to make us look like a joke."

"Just get it done," Ivan said.

"Excuse me, Mr. Morgan?"

Drake looked up to find Cole standing off to the side.

"May I speak with you please, sir?"

Drake excused himself from Gianna and his father and followed Cole outside the waiting room.

"I apologize for not being available this morning," Cole began. "I had some personal business to tend to."

"Never mind that," Drake said. "What's going on?"

"A week ago, I met privately with your brother. He asked me to look into Cecily Reed."

Drake shook his head in irritation. "I told him to let it go."

"Yes, sir, but like I told you, there wasn't much about her that I could give him. But there was something else I came across in my investigation. I took pictures and gave them to Leo. He said he was going to show them to you."

"That may have been why he wanted to meet with me. What were the pictures?"

"I brought copies," Cole said, pulling the photos from his pocket.

Drake flipped through the images, studied them and looked up at Cole.

"This is Tony Green," he said.

"Yes, sir," Cole confirmed.

Drake turned to eye Gianna who was inside the private waiting room, sitting beside his father and clutching his hand. As if she felt her eyes on him, she turned to look at Drake and Cole and gave him a questioning stare.

"You should also know that I just got word from one of my contacts in the SFPD that Mr. Green was found dead at his apartment."

Drake turned away from Gianna and studied the photos for a few more moments. Hours ago, he'd wanted Tony Green's address to pay him a visit. He was going there to ask the son of a bitch if he'd been working with Edmund to steal from the company. Now, he was dead, and his sister-in-law had apparently been meeting with him. There was no doubt in his mind now that this is why Leo wanted to see him. Now, Leo was in surgery, fighting for his life. Could Gianna have found out and…Jesus Christ.

"The police will be here any minute to take my statement. After that, I need to get back to the office and sort everything out," Drake said.

"What do you need from me?" Cole asked.

"Stay here and keep an eye on her. Don't let her anywhere near Leo. I'll be back later."

"Yes, sir," Cole said.

CHAPTER FORTY

"So, when I asked you where he was, and you told me no, that was a lie."

SAC Richard Santos glared at Cecily as she stood in Tony's small kitchen with her hip leaned against the counter. Several federal agents and law enforcement personnel crowded the apartment searching for any and everything that could be used for evidence in both the embezzlement case and Tony's murder. Cecily suggested his actual residence on the other side of town, but was informed Tony ended the lease on the apartment and moved out one year ago. It was more proof that he'd planned to get that money, leave town and never come back.

"I needed to see him, sir," Cecily said. "He betrayed me."

"And now he's dead, and you were the last one to see him alive."

"I told you what happened. He pulled a gun on me, left the apartment and then I heard shots downstairs. The perp was fleeing the scene just as I got downstairs. I gave chase, but he disappeared. I then called for an ambulance."

"That's it?"

She could feel the newspaper clipping burning a hole in her back pocket. She needed to get out of here, find Drake and ask him about it. This entire ordeal had been like one of Ivan Morgan's jigsaw puzzles. But finally, the pieces were beginning to fit, and a picture was forming. She just needed one last piece, and Drake was the one who could give it to her.

"Can I go now? I gave the officer on duty and one of the agents first on scene my statement," Cecily said. "I need to get home and prepare for my discipline hearing."

"You're still going to need to be debriefed," Richard said.

"Can it wait?"

"No," he erupted. "Because I have a dead former agent downstairs and an agent standing in front of me who I'm not sure I need to be arresting right now!"

The room grew quiet from his outburst, and Cecily glared at him. "I didn't kill him."

Richard breathed in and out and visibly calmed himself before stepping up to her and speaking in an undertone.

"This is out of my hands," he said. "You acted without guidance and accused a prominent figure in this community of embezzlement all on the word of a man who is no longer employed with this agency. Now he's dead, and my boss wants your head on a platter. Just come back to the office with me, and we'll go from there."

"You mean then you'll decide whether or not to arrest me," she concluded.

He stared at her in silence before one of the agents milling about called to him.

"Sir, there's a call for you from downtown."

Richard spared one last glance to Cecily and retreated to the bedroom to take his call. Cecily stared after him and mentally counted to five before she slipped past the SFPD cops and federal agents and out of the apartment.

CHAPTER FORTY-ONE

*D*rake sat on the sofa in his office, his gaze divided between the city lights and the photos of Gianna with Tony Green. He wondered, forlornly, if and when his life would ever return to normal.

"Why aren't you answering your phone?"

He turned his head to see Cecily rushing into the office, breathless. Her face was flushed, her hair and attire in disarray, but she still looked beautiful to him, and it only served to remind him of how goddamned good it felt to be with her. But he forced himself to shut that memory and every other memory with her off because he was sick of her hot and cold bullshit. This was the woman who had him arrested. After the months they spent together, she still believed the worst about him.

He turned his gaze back to the evening sky. "It's after hours. I just left the hospital, and I wanted peace and quiet."

"I heard about Leo," she said, coming to stand before him. "How is he?"

"He pulled through surgery, but he's still in a coma."

"I'm sorry, Drake."

Against his better judgment, he turned back to look at her. "Are you?"

"Of course, I am. He and I never got along, but he's your brother, and I know how much you love him."

He put the picture Cole had given him on the table face down and stood from the sofa to tower over her.

"Thank you, but I don't want your sympathy. I've had a hell of a day, and it seems like everyone I know is lying to me."

"I haven't lied to you."

"Then sit down and tell me everything I want to know."

"I will, but first there's something—"

"Sit down!"

She didn't flinch from his command, but her gaze turned steely and she slowly moved past him and sat down in the seat he just vacated.

"What do you want to know?" She asked.

"I heard Tony Green was killed tonight."

"That's right."

"And you were there?"

"Yes."

"Why?"

"Why do you think?" She asked. "I needed him to tell me to my face that he screwed me over."

"And did he?"

"More or less."

He stared at her and Cecily stared right back. "I didn't kill him," she said.

"I wasn't thinking that."

"Then why are you looking at me that way?"

"I'm trying to figure out how you're going to explain to your fellow agents that someone shot him, and you were the only one there. Do you know you're suspected of working with him?"

"My boss already suspects me, but it's not true. I never wanted or even cared about your money. I just wanted to put your brother and whoever he was working with behind bars. When I confronted Tony, he was on his way out of town. I was going to arrest him, but he pulled a gun on me and left. But someone killed him before he could get away."

She paused. "Someone with a strong motive."

He chuckled. "Now you're looking at me a certain way."

"He was stealing from you, and you already threatened to pay him a visit."

His jaw clenched. "If I had killed him, I'd gladly admit it, and I sure as hell wouldn't leave you there to take the fall."

Silence fell between them before Drake continued.

"Who was he to you?"

"We used to be partners at the Bureau. We also dated for a short while."

"I guessed as much," he said, determined to not let that point cloud his mind with jealousy. "What was his connection to Edmund?"

"He found out your brother was embezzling money; he got a job at the company and hatched a plan to relieve him of it. But Edmund found out Tony was a Fed. He must've thought Tony was trying to bring him down, so he put a price on his head and forced him to go into hiding."

"How did he know Edmund was stealing? How did the two of them even meet?" Drake asked.

"I don't know."

"Cecily—"

"I said I don't know, and that's the truth. Whatever he did to get himself inside the company, he didn't tell me. All this time, I thought he was working undercover, but that was a lie. When Edmund threatened his life, Tony had to leave, but he didn't want to give up all that money."

Drake began to slowly pace the length of his office back and forth. "Is that when he called you for help?"

"Yes. He knew I'd do anything for him, and he used that to get me to finish where he left off. He told me that even though it was an agency-sanctioned mission, his bosses didn't want him to pursue it—that it was a wild goose chase. He said he lost his reputation and finding that hidden account would get it back and prove to the agency that he was right all along. My job was to get proof of Edmund's embezzlement and arrest him."

"So, you come to me to get me to turn on my brother," he surmised.

"I told you. I thought I was conducting an actual investigation, and I needed a way inside the company. But then Edmund died, and things changed. Tony continued to lie to me. He told me no one at the agency would listen to him without proof of Edmund's crimes. We needed to find that hidden money. That's when I came up with the idea of us getting married."

Drake came to a halt in the middle of the room and glared at her.

Cecily sighed and continued. "With Edmund gone, it was the only way I could get close enough to your family and company to find that account. If I'd known Edmund had named you on the account, I would've—"

"What? Dropped the investigation?"

"I don't know, but what I do know is that I took on Tony's mission at his word when all he wanted was to steal the hundreds of millions in that account. He didn't have a problem with scapegoating me. Now, I'm up for disciplinary action at the agency."

He scoffed. "I hope you're not looking for sympathy. This is the man you chose to love and defend to me. Yet, all the while you couldn't see through your love that he didn't give a shit about you."

Cecily stood in a flash, and he guessed the truth in his words must've stung.

"You're right. I was a fool. But I'm trying to rectify all of that now. There's still a murderer out there, and I have a job to do."

Drake's thoughts zoomed to Gianna, but he couldn't tell Cecily about her until he was absolutely certain she was guilty.

"There's something you need to see," she said.

She pulled what looked to be a newspaper clipping from her back pocket and held it out for him to take it. Damn. Had she somehow already found out that Gianna was involved and this was the undeniable proof?

"Look at the picture," she insisted.

He hesitated and then took the picture she held out to him. He studied it, but when he realized what he was looking at, he frowned.

"Wait a minute," he said, pointing to the first man in the photograph. "That's Tony Green."

"Yes," she said.

His eyes trailed to the second man, and his brow deepened in confusion.

"You know who it is, don't you?" She asked.

"Yes, but—"

He looked up at her, but something else snagged his attention. A tall and broad figure came up quickly behind her and too late, Drake realized she was in danger.

"Cecily," he shouted and tried to move her out of the way.

But he wasn't quick enough. Something hard came down upon her head, and she fell limp and unconscious into his arms. Drake's eyes moved from Cecily's still form in his arms to meet the dark, penetrating eyes of his head of security.

"Pick her up and carry her downstairs to the car, Mr. Morgan," Cole said, aiming the gun at him. "It's time you and I had a meeting."

CHAPTER FORTY-TWO

*D*rake's heart pounded in his chest as the tires of the car hugged the road, taking him and Cole closer to the secluded cliffside spot he'd already designated. Cole, his eyes wild with a mix of desperation and madness, sat in the passenger seat, pressing the gun against Drake's side.

"I didn't want it to be like this, sir," Cole said. "I was going to take the money, disappear, and you'd never see me again. But Tony must've figured I'd sell him out, so he left clues for that bitch in the back seat to find."

Drake stole a quick glance in the rearview mirror. Cecily lay motionless in the back seat, unaware of the danger that surrounded her. His mind raced, and his instincts urged him to do whatever was needed to keep her safe. He figured the best way was to keep Cole's attention on him.

"You and Tony were working together?" Drake asked.

"From the beginning," Cole confirmed. "I knew your brother was stealing millions, and I came up with the idea to relieve him of it. Tony and I were in the Rangers together, and he was always smart as a whip. When we got out of the Army, we kept in touch, and I found out he was working for the FBI as some fancy accountant. He always bragged that if money was lost, he could find it. I told him what your brother was up to, and I didn't need to twist his arm to bring him on board."

"He led his superiors at the agency to believe that he was working on a different case while he went undercover as an accountant here at the company. He figured it wouldn't take long to find that account, funnel the money into another account he created and get out of dodge."

Cole snorted. "Everything was all good until Tony got too cocksure of himself. I told him to take it slow and not to underestimate Edmund. But he was found out. Edmund thought he was working undercover to take him down and put a price on Tony's head."

"Then Edmund died, and I thought with all the confusion and rearranging going on, Tony could get himself back into the company and continue the plan. But he feared Edmund's reach. Just because he was dead didn't mean the price on his head went away."

"So, he brought in Cecily," Drake guessed, just willing Cole to keep talking until he could find a way to overpower him and get Cecily to safety.

"He said she was a great forensic accountant and that she had some stupid crush on him and would do anything he said." Cole paused to shake his head ruefully. "Tony said she was good, but he underestimated just how good she was. She found the account in a matter of months."

"Did you stab Leo?"

"I had to. I had a feeling he was onto me," Cole said. "He wanted me to look into your fake wife just like you wanted me to look into Tony. I couldn't do either one, so I strung you both along with excuses and gave Leo a doctored photo of Gianna and Tony meeting to put his suspicions on her. Turns out, your brother is smarter than he looks."

The wind whipped through the open windows, carrying with it the salty scent of the nearby ocean. The road ahead curved, leading them closer to their destination. Drake's grip tightened on the steering wheel as his mind worked furiously to find a way out of the nightmare. Drake's eyes went to the rearview mirror again, and it startled him when he locked gazes with Cecily's open eyes. She slowly moved a finger to her lips, silently telling him not to give her away.

Cole's menacing words cut through the tension. "Once we're there, you're going to help me drag Cecily out of the car and toss her over that cliff. I'll shoot you in the back of the head, sir and make it painless."

Drake fought to keep his voice steady. "Cole, listen to me. You don't have to do this. Take the money, take my private jet and disappear."

Cole's eyes narrowed, his grip on the gun tightening. "I appreciate that, but Agent Reed won't stop until she finds me. From the moment Tony brought her in, I knew she'd be trouble. I knew she would never let us take those millions and disappear. I hid in her closet that night to watch her and see if I could get an angle on her, but I knew she wouldn't look the other way with Tony, and she definitely wouldn't with me. Once I'm done with you two, I'm going back to the hospital to finish off Leo. Then I'll disappear."

Suddenly, a jolt of energy surged through the car when Cecily kicked at the side of Cole's head. His body jerked forward, but his head missed the dashboard by only inches. On reflex, his hand shot up and the gun went off sounding like a canon in the enclosed space. Panic gripped Drake as he fought to maintain control of the vehicle, while Cecily dove toward the front console and tried to wrench the gun from Cole's hands.

During their struggle, Cecily's body hit the steering wheel and the car swerved violently, tires screeching against the asphalt. Drake reached over and plowed a fist into Cole's nose. Cole instantly loosened his hold on Cecily and Drake returned his eyes to the road and fought to regain control. But it was too late. The car crashed into a guard railing, and the impact sent it careening dangerously close to the edge of the cliff.

Cole regained his bearings and aimed his gun at Cecily. With a surge of strength, Drake lunged towards Cole, and the two of them fought in a deadly struggle for control of the gun while the car teetered on the edge of the cliff, its metal frame groaning in protest.

Desperation toiled through Drake as he fought to protect Cecily. With a final burst of strength, he knocked the gun from Cole's grip and punched him once then twice in the jaw. But it only temporarily disoriented the big man.

"Get out," Drake shouted to Cecily, as Cole now focused his attack on Drake.

As he fought to ward off Cole's counterattack, Drake saw Cecily stumble out of the car through the back window. She raced to the driver's side where he was, her eyes wide with terror. Cole's hands were now wrapped around Drake's throat. Drake's lungs begged for oxygen.

"When I'm done with you, I'm going to kill her," Cole gritted as his grip around Drake's neck tightened.

Then a shot rang out in the air and Cole was sent sprawling back against the passenger window. He gripped his right shoulder and blood seeped through his fingers. Drake took in several deep breaths of burning but welcome oxygen. He turned and saw that Cecily was still aiming her gun at Cole.

Cole's weight against the passenger side caused the car the rock further over the edge.

"Drake, get out of there," Cecily screamed.

She reached out and began to help him pull himself through the window. The car's balance was nearing its tipping point. Drake's attempt to escape caused it to tilt even further over the edge of the cliff to the watery abyss below.

"Come on," Cecily urged. "Push yourself!"

Drake's body was halfway through the window when he felt Cole's grasp on his leg pulling him back, trying to keep him trapped inside with him.

"No," Cecily screamed.

She reached past Drake and slammed the butt of the pistol against Cole's forehead, and Cole released him.

She then pulled with all her might and Drake pushed with determination to survive. His body strained, his muscles screamed in protest, but he refused to let go. With one final exertion of strength, Drake released himself from the car's grip and tumbled out. Together, he and Cecily fell to the rocky ground just as the car tilted one last time and spilled over the cliff.

Drake's heart thundered in his chest as he scrambled to his feet, pulling Cecily close to him. They stood at the rocky edge, watching as the car plummeted into the ravine below. The next thing they heard was the sound of metal crashing into the rocky landscape, coupled with Cole's terrified screams. Then in an instant, an explosion ripped through the air and flames erupted from the wreckage, casting an eerie glow across the desolate landscape.

CHAPTER FORTY-THREE

A week later, Leo woke from his coma. When he opened his eyes and set them on Drake, his father and Gianna standing around his bed, the first thing he rasped was, "Cole."

Drake nodded. "We got him. But how did you guess? The police said it was dark and no witnesses came forward to ID him."

"Jacket pocket," Leo rasped again.

Gianna stepped forward, lifted Leo's head and helped him eat some ice chips, while Drake went to the closet of his private hospital room to remove the suit jacket he'd been wearing the night he was stabbed. He dug into the inside of the lapel and withdrew a few black and white 5x7 inch photographs, unfolded them and saw the same images of Gianna meeting with former FBI agent, Tony Green.

"Before he died, he told me these were fakes." Drake looked at Leo. "You suspected they were fakes long before then?"

Leo nodded.

"How?"

"The date and time stamp is from a month ago," Gianna said. "And I'm still wearing my wedding ring in them."

Drake looked her way and then back to Leo who was nodding and confirming her words.

"Your brother always resented I took off Edmund's ring so soon after he died," she said, taking the pictures from Drake and looking them over. "Of course, he would be the one to notice something so small in a picture."

She paused to look up at Drake. "I hate that you suspected for even one moment that I would hurt Leo, much less steal from any of you. I wished you'd come to me."

Drake suddenly felt exhausted. "I'd gotten to a point where I didn't know who I could trust anymore." He turned to Leo. "Cole said he gave you these pictures to put suspicion on Gianna and get it off Cecily because she was the one finding the money."

"It was also just his way of putting less suspicion on himself," Leo said, softly. "He wanted it to look like everyone had a motive to kill Green, except him."

Drake shook his head in wonder and rubbed the top of Leo's head, mussing his hair. "Maybe you missed your calling as a Detective."

"If that's your way of firing me," Leo said, his eyes turning somber, "I'd understand. You'd be well within your rights to do just that."

"You're not going anywhere," Drake said adamantly. "There's been enough strife and tension in this family. I'll keep you on as COO, and maybe in a few months, we can talk about where you and I go from here."

Leo nodded and struggled to sit up. "Part of the reason I wanted you to meet me that night was to tell you that I canceled the deal with Gavin Reyes. If Cyrus or any of the other board members have a problem with it, they can come to me. I trust you, Drake, and I want this company's reputation turned around as much as you do."

He then mustered a smile which warmed Drake's heart. It had been a long time since he'd seen his brother smile. Then it was gone, as once again, Leo's face turned somber.

"I never should've blamed you for Edmund's death," he said. "I knew all along what he was doing." He looked at his father and Gianna. "We all knew what he was doing, but you were the only one with the courage to call him out on it. This is a family company, and he was stealing from our family, and I'm sorry for making you the enemy."

Drake nodded. "And while we're dishing out apologies, I'll add mine. I'm sorry I didn't tell you all about the arrangement I had with Cecily—I mean, Agent Reed. I didn't want to involve any of you, but again, we're a family, and I should've been open with all of you."

They lapsed into a comfortable silence as each Morgan processed the events of the past year—the betrayals, the secrets, and the murders. Drake prayed it was all over and that they could finally look to the future.

"I just have one question," Ivan said. "You and Cecily may have cooked all this up as a ruse, but I saw that marriage certificate, and it wasn't fake. So, tell me son, where's your wife?"

All eyes went to him, but Drake simply shrugged. "I'm sorry to disappoint you, Dad, but I had my lawyer send her the annulment papers yesterday morning. She won't be my wife for much longer."

Silence fell for a moment and then Leo spoke. "That's a shame. I liked her."

With that, the room erupted in laughter.

* * *

An hour later, Drake left Leo's hospital room, closed the door behind him and turned to find Elise walking up, her hands full with her purse and a bouquet of flowers.

"Hi," she said.

"Hey," he replied and motioned with his thumb to the closed door. "The family is in there. They'll be glad to see you."

He started to move past her, but she blocked his way.

"I miss you, Drake," she said. "I think I'll always care about you, but I see now that you were right. I'm not in love with you. I was just in love with your life."

"It's all right," he said. "Many people are."

Elise nodded and then hesitated. "Is she?"

Drake chuckled but to him it sounded forced. "No. She might be the first person I've met who isn't impressed by it."

"That must've been nice for you." She hesitated again. "Listen, I owe you an apology. I told Leo about seeing you with Cecily a year ago. I didn't know you two were working together to take down Edmund, and I should've just kept it to myself."

"It's all right," he said. "Everything worked out."

"No, don't let me off so easily. You told me you had an arrangement with her, but my jealousy and fear of me losing access to you and your life wouldn't allow me to just fall back. I gave him ammunition to take away your CEO title."

Drake held up a hand. "Leo and I have a lot of work to do to mend our relationship, but we'll get there. As for my title, I'm back in charge, so don't worry about that anymore."

He then gently held her forearm in comfort. "Like my family, I kept you in the dark. I wish I could go back and be honest with all of you, but I was ashamed and feeling guilty about betraying Edmund even though he deserved it. So please, stop beating yourself up, especially since I caused all this."

Elise glanced down at his hand on her arm and then up at him. She stepped closer, inched herself higher in her heels and planted a soft kiss on the side of his face.

"You're a good man, Drake Morgan."

She moved past him, put her hand to the doorknob of Leo's room and then paused to turn back to him once more.

"I know you love Cecily. As many times as you denied it to me, I couldn't deny it to myself. I could see it in the way you looked at her."

Discomfort ran through him, and he shrugged with a mask of indifference. "Maybe, but it's one-sided. I can't chase after her anymore."

"You said your wealth doesn't impress her?"

"That's right," he confirmed. "Flaunting my money isn't the way to get her attention."

For a second, Elise seemed to be lost in thought. "That's funny, especially when she's wearing that one-of-a-kind opal around her neck."

A frown creased Drake's brow. "What are you talking about?"

"That necklace she wears," she clarified. "I noticed it when I came to your house that night."

"Oh, that," he said, nodding in recognition. "Yeah, she wears it everywhere, but she usually keeps it tucked underneath her shirt."

"Well, that night, it was on full display. It's a rare opal. They only made about five of them in the world. Trust me, I know my rare gems."

Drake continued to frown as his mind began to race with each word she spoke. "It's her birthstone."

Elise chuckled. "Well, that particular birthstone she's wearing is worth about a half a million dollars."

CHAPTER FORTY-FOUR

One month later…

Cecily planted her bare feet in the sand and braced herself as the cold water of the tide rushed in, covered her feet and just as quickly, rejoined the sea. She looked around and inhaled the salty air. It was a good a place to think—and escape.

"You look different today."

She turned behind her and saw Drake coming down the boardwalk from his beach house. His suit jacket was gone, and his dress shirt was untucked from his trousers with the top button undone. He gestured to her casual attire of loose jeans rolled up at the ankles and a snug peach-colored t-shirt.

"It's my day off," she said, tucking wind-blown strands of hair behind her ear. "What's your excuse?"

"As soon as my meeting ended, I called it a day."

"I didn't hear a chopper landing," she quipped.

He smiled. "I drove myself. I like the view of the coastline. Thanks for coming."

She shrugged. "It's a beautiful place. It gave me the chance to thank you in person for the call you made to my bosses. The Bureau has agreed to overlook my actions in working with Tony."

"My pleasure. I didn't want to see you lose your job. You're too good at it, and I can see you love what you do. But to be honest, I'm sure they recognized how valuable you are. No one else would've been able to find where Green stashed that money but you."

She smiled, knowingly and continued. "Also, I guess I should've started with this, but thank you for saving my life."

"You don't ever have to thank me for that."

The wind picked up speed between them, but she could still feel his closeness, and it unnerved her.

She took a step back. "About Tony…"

"I didn't invite you out here to talk about your boyfriend. I said some things that were cruel—"

"But they were the truth," she finished. "You were right. He didn't love me, but I let my feelings for him blind me to what he was really after, and it caused a shitstorm not just with my career but within your company. I'm sorry for that."

Their eyes connected.

"Is that all you want to say to me?" He asked.

She had so much she wanted to say to him. But the coward in her told her to keep quiet and reserve those words for her daydreams.

She shrugged with masked indifference. "That's it. Why did you want to see me? Didn't your lawyer get the annulment papers?"

"Yes."

"Don't tell me you're cashing in another raincheck?"

"Not exactly." He reached into his pocket, pulled out a sealed envelope and handed it to her. "This is for you."

Cecily hesitated but then took the envelope out of his hands and slowly tore it open. Before she could finish reading the document in its entirety, a lump built up in her throat.

"Drake," was all she could say on a heavy sigh filled with emotion.

She folded the paper and tucked it in her back pocket. Then she looked to the ocean, wishing she could float away with the waves. How? How did he always find a way to penetrate her heart?

"You shouldn't have done this."

"You deserve to know where they're buried, so I had my investigators find out."

She turned to look at him head on as resentment and anger rose within her. She didn't really resent him, and she wasn't at all angry with him. It was just that anger was good because it kept her deeper, raw feelings for him at bay.

"Did you ever think I didn't want to know?"

"Why? Because you're still carrying around that guilt? You didn't kill them, Cecily. You had nothing to do with their deaths. You were a child and life gave you a bad card early on. None of this is your fault."

"That's so easy for you to say with the family and the business—"

"Yeah, I'm lucky," he interrupted stepping close to her and invading her space, "and I'm not going to apologize for it. I'm also not going to hide it like you."

She stilled. Her anger was quickly washed away with the tide only to be replaced with trepidation.

"What are you talking about?"

"That wasn't all I wanted to do for you. I wanted to buy that rec center from the city, but that didn't work out."

Cecily turned away from him to stare into the blue waters again and silently prayed to God he would just let this go.

"It would've been a nice gesture, but again, not necessary," she said.

"Yeah, I even put in an offer, but it seems I was outbid by someone."

She could feel his eyes boring into her, but she refused to look at him and kept her attention fixed on the water.

"But you see, I'm a sore loser," he continued. "So, I had to find out who outbid me and make sure it wasn't some corporation buying the building just to bulldoze it and build expensive condos."

Silence.

"Cecily. Look at me."

She closed her eyes and heaved a sigh. She then opened them and slowly turned to face him, realizing that this was Drake. Of course, he already knew the truth about her.

"You know, after Cole confessed everything to me that night, it got me thinking that maybe he never ran a background check on you at all. He said he was just stringing me along, so I started to assume that everything he gave me about you was basic information anyone could've gotten. He might have just been regurgitating facts you probably told Tony."

"So, this time, you conducted the background check yourself," she surmised.

"Again, with the help of my investigators."

She brushed wisps of her hair from her face and stood there with her feet planted in the sand as he divulged facts about her she'd done her best to keep hidden.

"You go by Cecily Reed, which is your late father's last name. But you were adopted when you turned twelve, and your legal name is Cecily Atwood. Your adopted father is Charles Atwood, who people called a genius in the optics field. He and his wife Elaine couldn't have children of their own, so they adopted you, raised you and loved you. When they tragically passed, you inherited a controlling share in his business and a trust fund worth nearly 300 million dollars."

"Those adoption records were sealed," she said.

"Yeah, well I'm Drake Morgan." He paused to shake his head as if in wonder. "But even I didn't expect that. When I found out, my first thought was you were a hypocrite. You never wasted a moment to throw my wealth into my face when all this time you were a wealthy woman yourself. But then I saw you never touched that money or sold those shares. You ignored it all until now—when you bought the rec center."

"I should've done it a long time ago," Cecily said. "If I wasn't so pig-headed about that stupid money, those kids could've had better. I don't care anything about that money. I don't even want it."

"Why?"

She chuckled with self-disparagement. "Charles and Elaine Atwood didn't buy my bratty act. They saw it for what it was which was me trying to reject them. But they loved me anyway. The truth was I loved them, too. But six years ago, Charles had a severe heart attack and died. Elaine, died in her sleep a year later. My guess is she was too heartbroken to live without him."

Drake pulled her necklace from underneath her shirt. "You said this was a gift, but all this time, I thought it was a gift from your birth parents. The Atwood's gave this to you, didn't they?"

She took the necklace out of his hands and clutched it. "It was the day the adoption went through, and I officially became an Atwood."

"You know how much it's worth?"

"Yes, and I don't care."

Tears brimmed in her eyes, but she viciously swiped them away before they could fall.

"I don't care about any of this stuff. I never wanted their money or the company. I just wanted my parents back, and I wanted Charles and Elaine back. So even though I can't stop thinking about you, even though I imagine us going on dates to fancy restaurants, making love in your over-the-top Presidential suite in Olympus, or just cuddled on the couch and binge-watching tv together, I'm not going to do it because everyone I love leaves me!"

He took hold of her shoulders, forcing her to keep her eyes on him.

"I never knew you to be scared of anything. Don't be scared of this. I love you. That day you disturbed my lunch, I told you to never contact me again, but I didn't mean it. I wanted to see you again, and again."

"Please stop!" She raised her voice above the crashing and roaring waves. "You don't need—"

"You're right! I don't need anything," he shouted above her. "But I do need you!"

She shook herself free of his grasp and started to march off. She had to get away from him and his declarations of love. But Drake jogged up to her and whisked her around.

"Don't run away from me."

"I can't stand here and listen to you say you have feelings for me, because it's ridiculous. I don't belong in your world. I came into your family to find Edmund's stolen money and give it back to your company. That's done. It's over."

"It doesn't mean we have to be over," he argued. "Your world, my world, who gives a fuck? I want to be with you, and I know you want to be with me, too."

"Drake, please stop. I can't allow myself to fall in love with you."

"We don't have to live in the mansion, and I'll sell this beach house. We don't even have to take the jet when we go on vacation. I'll fly coach with you if that's what you want, while we both pretend we don't have enough to buy the entire damn airline."

Cecily gaped at him and then suddenly, unexpected laughter bubbled up from deep inside her and exploded without warning. It surprised them both and for several moments, she was overcome with giggles.

"I'm sorry," she said, wiping tears of mirth from her eyes. "I just can't picture you flying coach."

Suddenly, Drake let out a laugh and the two of them laughed hysterically at the image of him sitting in the coach section with ordinary Joes and Janes.

"You look amazing when you laugh," he said. "You should do it more often."

Her laughter subsided, and he reached out and whisked strands of hair from her face. "I'll do whatever you want if you're there with me. I didn't want to fall in love with you, Cecily. I tried to convince myself I despised you because seeing you only made me think of having to turn my brother in for being a thief. But the truth is, you got to me the moment I saw you."

"You know what I want to hear, don't you?" He asked.

She knew exactly what he wanted to hear. She told her parents many times she loved them and then they died. So, she stopped saying the words out loud. She loved Charles and Elaine dearly, but never told them and they were still taken from her. And the truth is, she absolutely loved the man standing in front of her. But what if she uttered the words and...

"I'm not going anywhere," he promised as if reading her thoughts. "Say it, Cecily."

Fresh tears stung her eyes and this time she let them fall. "You were the only one who made me forget about Tony. Just that one night with you in Houston made me realize I could love someone else besides him. It scared me. And then being married to you, I kept trying to convince myself I didn't feel anything for you when I really did. But I could never admit it, because I was afraid."

He framed her face with his hands. "Dammit, Cecily, just say it."

A gust of wind swept between them, but they stood there together as she decided to once again, risk her heart. She spoke the words on a whisper but loud enough for only him to hear before they were carried away by the wind and out to sea.

"I love you. I love you, Drake."

He brought her into him and kissed her until they were both breathless. They ravaged each other, moaned for each other. When they were both overcome with wanting, Drake took her by the hand and practically dragged her up the walkway toward the beach house.

"Don't sell this place," she said.

"I wasn't going to," he said, turning back to look at her with a wink.

"It'll be hell travelling back and forth to the city for work," she said.

"We can move into your tiny condo tomorrow."

When they got to the house, he unlocked the front door and turned to lift her by the waist. "Right now, we need a bed, and this is the closest one."

He carried her inside and stole another kiss before kicking the door shut behind them.

* * *

Thank you for reading EXTORTION! I hope you enjoyed Drake and Cecily's exciting love story. If you love romantic suspense and mystery, be sure to read all the books in the Ex Files series with the Ex Files Box Set.

ONE-CLICK EX FILES BOX SET NOW >
"I love this series!"
"True romantic suspense!"

SIGN UP FOR LISA'S NEWSLETTER:
www.lisaryancampbell.com/newsletter

And if you love a springtime romance with suspense, make sure you check out EX APPEAL, an EX FILES novella.

Ava never thought she'd return to Gypsy Bay, but she did and her job is to investigate the unsolved murder of Michelle Meyer. But all the evidence is pointing to one person and the reason Ava left town in the first place…Michelle's husband.

"Loved, loved, loved this book!"

"Loved the suspense, danger, twists and turns!"

"I haven't been this intrigued by a book for awhile…this was phenomenal!"

ONE-CLICK EX APPEAL for a steamy and suspenseful read.

ABOUT THE AUTHOR

Award-winning Author, Lisa Ryan Campbell began writing as a small child using her mother's pink typewriting paper. Years later, she decided it was important to get a "real job" and attended Arizona State University to major in English with the goal of continuing on for both a Master's and Doctorate degrees in English and teach at the college level.

In 2002, Lisa graduated with a Bachelor's degree in English Literature and an Ancient Egyptian romance novel she wrote in her spare time. She decided then she would not be continuing on to graduate school, but instead joined Romance Writers of America and focused on her true love.

Lisa is an avid traveler and has seen many of the world's treasures in Egypt, Peru, Spain, France, Morocco, England, Mexico and the Caribbean. She spends her time mostly at her home in Colorado writing, reading and watching 1940's noir movies. She also loves to laugh, so you may frequently catch her watching reruns of Archer, Veep and The Office.

Sign up for Lisa's newsletter and find out more about her books at www.Lisaryancampbell.com and connect with her on social media.